KILLING TOWN
A MIKE HAMMER NOVEL

KILLING TOWN

A MIKE HAMMER NOVEL

MICKEY SPILLANE
and
MAX ALLAN COLLINS

TITANBOOKS

Killing Town: A Mike Hammer Novel
Hardback edition ISBN: 9781785655500
E-book edition ISBN: 9781785655517
Mass-market paperback edition ISBN: 9781789093421

Published by Titan Books
A division of Titan Publishing Group Ltd
144 Southwark Street
London SE1 0UP

First mass-market edition: April 2020

1 3 5 7 9 10 8 6 4 2

This is a work of fiction. Names, characters, places, and incidents
either are the product of the author's imagination or are used fictitiously,
and any resemblance to actual persons, living or dead, business
establishments, events, or locales is entirely coincidental. The publisher
does not have any control over and does not assume any responsibility for
author or third-party websites or their content.

Mickey Spillane and Max Allan Collins assert the moral right to be
identified as the authors of this work.

A CIP catalogue record for this title is available from the British Library.

Printed and bound in the United States.

Did you enjoy this book? We love to hear from our readers.
Please email us at readerfeedback@titanemail.com or write to us at
Reader Feedback at the above address.

To receive advance information, news, competitions, and exclusive
Titan offers online, please sign up for the Titan newsletter on
our website: www.titanbooks.com

FOR MICKEY

Happy birthday, buddy

MEET MIKE HAMMER
AN INTRODUCTION
BY MAX ALLAN COLLINS

I have told the story numerous times since Mickey Spillane's passing in 2006. If you've heard this before, perhaps more than once, skip ahead as much as you like… but be careful. There are surprises coming. This is a book with Mickey Spillane's name on it, after all.

In the final week of his life, Mike Hammer's creator said to his wife Jane, "When I'm gone, there'll be a treasure hunt around here. Take everything you find and give it to Max. He'll know what to do."

Mickey had already called me, a week before, asking me to finish the Mike Hammer novel, *The Goliath Bone*, if he was unable to.

I had been Mickey's fan since the early sixties, when as an adolescent I'd discovered his fever-dream prose. I was led there by the Darren McGavin TV series (*Mickey Spillane's Mike Hammer*, 1958–1959). The late fifties and early sixties saw a wave of private eye TV shows, with the Hammer imitation *Peter Gunn* leading the pack, its creator Blake Edwards having written and directed a failed *Hammer* TV pilot.

I became a fanatic about Spillane, whose noir poetry mingled with a level of sex and violence unavailable in other mysteries of the day, exploding my thirteen-year-old skull into fragments as if by Hammer's .45 automatic. Within a year I was writing Spillane-style stories and sending them in the mail to publishers, none of whom seemed to be looking for teenaged mystery writers.

But I began publishing by the early 1970s and, along the way, became known as Spillane's defender—though he was the most popular American mystery writer of the twentieth century, Mickey's work has been attacked with a fervor unparalleled in American letters. He was blamed for juvenile delinquency and for ruining the reading habits of adults, too. *The Atlantic* eviscerated him and so did *Parents' Magazine*; self-righteous shrink Dr. Frederic Wertham singled out Spillane in his anti-comic book screed, *Seduction of the Innocent* (1954), the only writer of prose fiction to be so vilified.

Because I'd written articles defending and praising Spillane, I was invited to be the liaison between him and the 1981 Bouchercon (the major mystery fan convention, named for *New York Times* critic Anthony Boucher, who was among the first wave of Spillane's attackers). Held in Milwaukee, the con was tying into that city's beer persona by having Spillane, then starring in very clever and successful TV commercials for Miller Lite, as a guest of honor.

I had written Mickey perhaps one-hundred fan letters, but the only one he answered was in 1973, when I sent him my first published novel (*Bait Money*), and he welcomed me to the professional community of writers. So when I was introduced to Mickey, he said, "Oh, I know Max! We've been corresponding for years." And I said, "That's right, Mickey—one-hundred letters from me, one letter from you."

And we became fast friends.

This led to me visiting him, from time to time, in his home at Murrells Inlet, South Carolina. I was there when he met Jane Rogers, who would become his wife (well, he'd first known her when she was a little kid before she moved away). He accepted when I asked him to be my son Nathan's godfather. We collaborated on numerous projects together, including anthologies, an early 1990s comic book series (*Mike Danger*, a science-fiction private eye), and a biographical documentary (*Mike Hammer's Mickey Spillane*, 1999, featured on the Criterion DVD/Blu-ray of the great Hammer noir, *Kiss Me Deadly*).

During my visits to South Carolina, we would talk writing. He had many friends in that part of the world, but no writer friends. He liked to talk shop. Deep into the night, he would share with me his plans for various Mike Hammer novels, often acting out the wild endings that were his trademark. On one visit, he sent two one-hundred-page-plus unfinished Hammer manuscripts home with me for safekeeping, as if prescient about Hurricane Hugo, which would soon destroy his home.

With my wife Barb—she and I write the "Antiques" mystery series together, as "Barbara Allan" (*Antiques Wanted*)—I went down to Murrells Inlet for a special post-funeral celebration of Mickey's life. We stayed on to go through the many stacks of unpublished material that Mickey had left behind. For days, Barb, Jane, and I sat around the big Spillane dining room table—piled with stacks of manuscript pages—and would sort through. Now and then someone would shout, "I've got a Hammer!"

Why Mickey left behind so many unfinished works—particularly since his prose was so valuable commercially—cannot be answered simply. Part of it had to do with his religious conversion to the conservative Jehovah's Witnesses, who at least twice disenfranchised him due to the level of sex and violence in his work. In other words, Mickey Spillane's Church told him to quit writing like Mickey Spillane. They did not, however, ask him to quit tithing.

But there were other factors. Mickey often had more than one novel going—he would get "stuck" on one, and turn to another. Also, he loved doing beginnings and endings—and no one in the genre was ever better at either—but sometimes got bored in the middle. His favorite form was the 20,000-word novelette, and he spent almost a decade at the height of his fame writing them for low-end men's magazines that paid him a pittance. His fertile imagination sometimes worked against him—he'd get a new idea, and set aside a manuscript to pursue it.

Unlike Agatha Christie, Rex Stout, and Erle Stanley Gardner—his contemporaries—Mickey did not write scores of novels about his famous character. There are around one-hundred Perry Mason novels, but Mickey published only thirteen Mike Hammer novels. This made the half-dozen significant Hammer manuscripts—again, usually in the one-hundred-page range—such an exhilarating find.

One particularly brittle, discolored manuscript—in the treasure hunt Jane, Barb, and I conducted (beautiful women are always around when Mike Hammer is involved)—stirred my memory. *Mickey had shown this one to me!* It had been special to him.

On my visits to his Murrells Inlet home, late at night, we would repair to his third-floor office—he had two others on the now rebuilt property—and we would talk writing. In particular, he would regale me with ideas he had for future Mike Hammer novels. The subdued lighting invoked the beachfront campfires where young lifeguard Frank Morrison Spillane would "scare hell out" of his friends with spooky stories; but that lighting also had an appropriately noir flavor.

After all, we were talking Mike Hammer.

It was in that office, during one bull session, that he shared with me the endings for *King of the Weeds*, *The Big Bang*, and *Kiss Her Goodbye*—novels in progress that I would have been astonished to learn would eventually be completed by me... including putting Mickey's mesmerizing endings into prose.

On one such occasion, he withdrew from somewhere—like Bugs Bunny summoning a carrot or a machine gun—a browning, crumble-edged, fairly lengthy manuscript. It ran about thirty dense single-spaced pages, the equivalent of sixty-some double-spaced pages. I began reading.

"You wrote this a long time ago," I said.

He had pulled up a chair, turned it backward and sat, studying me, wearing a devilish, little-kid smile that threatened to turn to laughter at any moment. He nodded.

I kept reading. "This is good."

Soft chuckle. "I know." That laugh-threatening smile. "Is this what I *think* it is?"

A sly nod. The smile continued.

For half an hour, he sat enjoying me enjoy what was clearly an early appearance of Mike Hammer. But it was different from anything else about Hammer I'd read—he was even more of a lone wolf. Velda wasn't his secretary yet. He was doing an undercover job in a small, corrupt town. Some of the flavor of the famous early non-Hammer, *The Long Wait*, permeated the ancient pages.

"This is terrific," I said, when I'd breathlessly raced through the chapters. "Where does it go from here?"

He shrugged, collected the pages, stowed them somewhere, and we moved onto other subjects.

In the surprising wealth of unfinished Hammer novels and short stories we discovered, two stood out as something really special. All were interesting, and several were recent, including his final Hammer, *The Goliath Bone*, and the penultimate *King of the Weeds*. Several others were clearly "comeback" books—novels that would reintroduce the famous detective after a sustained absence, as in the disco-era *Kiss Her Goodbye*.

But these other two manuscripts were really, really old, interior evidence dating them to early in the post-World War II period—around 1945. *Lady, Go Die!* had revealed itself as the second Mike Hammer story, the unfinished sequel to *I, the Jury*. Yet this other manuscript indicated *I, the Jury* itself was the second Mike Hammer story.

Killing Town (as I have called it—Mickey's pages bore no title) indeed appeared to be the first Mike Hammer novel.

To me, it seemed exceptionally strong, but the absence of Manhattan, Velda and Pat Chambers made it somewhat atypical, and Hammer himself was not as vengeance-driven as in the later novels, though he was as hardboiled as ever. What to do with this special tough-guy pulp jewel?

As it happened, Mickey's last completed novel, *The Last Stand*, was also not a typical work—for one thing, it was a modern-day western that didn't feature Hammer at all. I found it quite wonderful. But in 2006, preparing a program of Spillane novels developed from his files required (it seemed to me) starting with full-blown Mike Hammer stories. And he had left something like a dozen of those, six substantial, six more shorter but significant, not to mention even shorter fragments that became the short stories collected in *A Long Time Dead*.

What to do with these two very special works?

That's when it occurred to me that saving both of them for the centenary of Mickey's 1918 birth would be perfect timing. Fortunately, Titan Books agreed with me. They, and their associate publisher, Hard Case Crime, were keen to celebrate Mickey's day (a day of the guns, as it were) with the publication of the last solo Spillane novel, and the very first Mike Hammer story.

Which you hold in your hands.

For purposes of continuity, we will assume this tale takes place in 1946 or '47, around a year before the events of *I, the Jury*. This is a Mike Hammer younger than we've seen, a recent veteran of combat in the Pacific, a raw, aggressive roughneck, minus the somewhat civilizing influence of his secretary/ partner Velda, the strong female equal he has not yet met. You are cautioned to keep in mind that this is a story begun and conceived over seventy years ago by a writer who was about to rock the conventions of popular culture with a new level of violence and sexual content. You are advised to drop all notions of political correctness in the basket at the door before entering the Mickey Spillane Theater.

And don't worry. There will be at least two more Mike Hammer mysteries… but they will have to wait for the next hundred years.

Max Allan Collins
September 9, 2017

CHAPTER ONE

The blonde dame in the sleeper car window was damn near naked in front of the mirror on the back of her closed door, and ready to finish the job. She hadn't bothered to pull down the shade, maybe because her train was in the yards backed up on a curve of track against a stalled freight.

And she didn't know she had company, by way of somebody catching a ride under that freight.

I didn't catch what she was changing out of—she was stark naked soon enough, and not a natural blonde but nobody's perfect. Right now she was climbing into some black lacy stuff, several pieces of it, including the sheer black nylons she was hooking to the garter belt, shapely right leg lifted with the toes stretching out. Then this very grown woman with baby-doll features stood there pirouetting around while she brushed out her hair, making love to her reflection but good.

For once I wasn't in the mood to enjoy a candid strip act, and anyway I was no peeping Tom—just a tag-along passenger working the cricks out of a back stiff from accommodations under the box car, aching all over from where sharp-edged pebbles had bounced off. A hunk of baling wire between the tracks had ripped a furrow down my pant leg, and the cloth flapped around the gash until I got in my battered overnight case and got a safety pin to clip the tears together. At least the gash wasn't in me.

And maybe, doing that, I caught a few more glimpses of the babe in the window. Just maybe.

There was dirt caked in the stubble of my beard and ground into my scalp. My hands and face must have been as black as the night itself, its sultry heat sending rivulets of sweat down that turned it into pure muck. Travel under a train does not come with shower facilities. My preening beauty wouldn't have found much to look at where I was concerned.

Somebody else would find me worth looking at, though. Down the line I could hear the yard cops flushing out the bums, nightsticks making dull, soggy noises where they landed. Sometimes sharper, cracking sounds were followed by hoarse screams and a torrent of curses, mixed in with the rumbles and bangs and whines of trains moving and braking and bumping.

Then they were closing in from both ends and I was

ready to kick the first guy in the chops who stuck his face in between the cars where I was standing. For a minute there was a lull, and I was just about to make a break for it when the beam of a flash split the night in half and light bounced off from somewhere, catching brass buttons not twenty feet away.

The big tough bull in blue looked like he was frozen there, staring straight at me.

I pressed back into the shadows trying to hug the rear of the car. I was jammed up against the steel ladder that ran to the top, wishing I dared move and get the overnight case in my hand turned around so it wouldn't make such a conspicuous bulge. Same went for the packet tucked in the front of my shirt under my old field jacket.

Damn it to hell—*he was waiting for me to come out so he could get a clear swing at me!* It hadn't taken me long to regret leaving my .45 behind.

Behind me I could half-sense the dame snugging into her undies, but I would have liked it better if she had switched out the light. It was turning me into a silhouette that couldn't be missed unless that guy had left some thick glasses at home.

I was all set to pitch out that bag in the railroad cop's kisser, to take some teeth and make a break for it, when I realized the copper wasn't in the same mood as me—not by a long shot. More lights came by, hitting his face, and this time I saw his eyes. No, they weren't looking at me at all. They went right by me to the dame in the sleeper-car window, and I could have lit a butt without him seeing the match. Could have started in blowing smoke rings, too.

What the hell? The curve of track gave me a vantage point, so I took one last look at her myself.

She was working on the other nylon now, toes stretched out ballet-style, and then her feet found the floor and she had a look at herself too, probably thinking Gypsy Rose Lee had nothing on her. Her red-nailed hands cupped this and that and her chin lifted, her mouth all white teeth and crimson lipstick and pure confidence. She was having a hell of a good time in front of that mirror. Hell of a good time.

But I needed to get out of there while the railroad officer was still getting his fill.

I slid off into the alley between the freight and the sleeper, ducked under the light and walked to the end of the string of cars. I didn't have a bit of trouble after that. Just strolled out of the yards into the passenger station, cleaned up in the restroom, dumping the torn trousers and glad I'd brought a few changes along.

Then I went down a dingy, ill-lit, worse-smelling street to a sloppy hash house crowded with a section gang going on late shift. I ate at the counter and a cute waitress with black streaks in her blonde hair and pretty green eyes flirted with me as she took my order for bacon and eggs. She was twenty going on forty.

"You just roll into town, mister?"

She didn't know how right she was.

"Yeah. My first trip to Rhode Island. What do I need to know about this burg?"

"Killington? More like Killing Town—it'll kill your dreams deader than a mackerel. And does this burg know about dead mackerels!"

Her joke missed me, but I gave her a grin anyway.

She went over to the kitchen window. She had a nice shape and when she stepped on her tiptoes to shout the order in, her fanny said hello. Five minutes later she was back with my food and a refill of my coffee.

"Where you from?" she asked.

"New York."

"The big town! Man, would I like to get there some time."

"Not that far away, sugar."

"A world away from here."

I threw down the plate of bacon and eggs, left her a buck tip, then went out and roamed around until I found a hotel one step up from a flophouse.

The bleary-eyed night clerk, looking forty and probably not thirty, was smoking a cigarette that didn't have tobacco in it. His shirt had been white once and his bow tie was half off, hanging like a carelessly picked scab. He shoved the register at me without really looking. I wrote "Hammer, Mike," and passed over my buck. For that I got a key to a closet masquerading as a room where I dumped my bag before I came downstairs again.

When the clerk saw me, he did his best to place me, then made me as his new arrival and reluctantly let go of the smoke he was holding in his lungs, also letting out a few words: "Want a whore?"

Full service, this place.

I said no thanks and pitched my key on the desk.

Some town, Killington.

Two doors down from the hotel through the rank-smelling night waited a cellar bar that hadn't done anything to itself since Prohibition except get a license. The walls were bare brick with only a couple inches of clearance over my head. An old scarred mahogany bar ran along one side while a few tables were spaced around the rest of the room, wearing so many scratches they at first seemed covered with patterned cloths.

A pair of sharp articles played blackjack at one table; two frowsy, blousy women with shrill voices and ugly print dresses had another; and over in the corner a kid about twenty sat at one having a quiet argument with his girl. Neither of them belonged in the place. They had good manners and good clothes, and from the flush on the girl's face and the excitement that showed in her eyes, it was a slumming party with the skirt doing the picking.

Probably this was her way of telling her boy friend she was up for anything—get it? *Anything.* Psychology, it's called.

Over the bar was a clock that said it was a quarter after one. Two and a half hours since the naked babe on the train. In the upper corner of the mirror over the back bar was a bullet hole spider-webbed with cracks. Place had character, all right.

I sat there and filled up on beer. I was dry right down to my shoes from the trip from Manhattan to Rhode Island on the rods, and until I had three brews under my belt, I didn't get anything but wet. But don't let anybody tell you that you can't get drunk on beer. On six I was mellow, and one later I was there.

The street door opened and let in some more of the humid night. For a minute the brunette just looked the place over, her almond-shaped brown eyes taking everything in, her full mouth wearing lipstick so red it was almost black. She nearly changed her mind about coming in, then shrugged and walked over on her black high-heeled strappy pumps to the bar.

It wasn't exactly a walk—there should have been an orchestra, a stage and wings for her to come out of. She was nicely stacked, shades of blue-and-pink jersey dress clinging as if she were facing a headwind. All that brown hair bounced off her shoulders while she held her stomach in to keep her breasts high and breathed through a faint smile that might have been real if it weren't so damned professional.

Sure, she picked me. Maybe she could sense class when she saw it. Or maybe she liked the color of my dough on the bar. The other two drunks were showing nickels and dimes while I sported change of a twenty.

The greasy, glassy-eyed bartender, two parts pockmark and one part skimpy mustache, swabbed down the bar in front of her with a wet rag, looking like he could use a swabbing himself. "What'll it be, honey?" he gruffed.

Her eyes passed over the Scotch bottles, but she said tiredly, "Whiskey and ginger."

I kicked a buck forward. "Make it Scotch. Best you got. Soda on the side."

Hell, why waste time.

The brunette raised her eyebrows and smiled at me. "Well… thank you. You know, I don't usually…"

"Skip it, sis," I said. "I was already in the mood for company." I finished my current beer, watching her over the rim of the glass.

She shrugged and the smile looked a little tired, too. "Does it show on me that much?"

I put the glass down and let the bartender fill it up again. "Not really," I lied.

"Couldn't I just be some lonely girl looking for a nice guy?"

"Maybe, but you didn't find one." I shrugged. "You look just fine. I'm just used to spotting the symptoms."

Her sigh was abrupt and so were the words that followed: "Someday I'm going to get out of this town and get a real job."

"What's the matter with the one you got?"

If I had been leering, she would have given me the glass of booze right in the face. But I wasn't leering, so she studied me curiously a moment. "Don't see a ring. You married?"

"Nope."

"Got any kids?"

I grinned. "Not that I know of."

She swirled the ice around in her glass. "Want to hear something funny?"

"Sure."

She looked in the mirror behind the bar, past her reflection. "I want both. A ring and kids. Together and legitimately."

"So what are you doing about it?"

Her shoulders made that resigned motion again. "Not much. Anyway, men like *nice girls*, don't they?"

"Like women like nice guys? That one was started by an old maid who died a virgin. You can have your nice girls. They're all a pack of phonies."

The sleepy, one-hiked-eyebrow glance she gave me was deliberately sarcastic. "Really?"

"I mean it," I said. "They're phonies because they're all liars. Everyone wants the same things and the good girls are afraid to go after it."

"Which is what?"

"Sex. Money. Not necessarily in that order. So they think up lies to excuse themselves, get loaded down with frustrations that turn into inhibitions, and when they finally do get married and give it up? The first thing you know, the Holy Union is on the rocks."

"That right?"

"That's right. Hell, give me a dame that knows her way around every time. When *they* settle down, they're *really* settled and know how to treat a guy. Like I said, the nice girls you can have."

"Thanks." Her eyes were laughing at me. I ordered her another drink. "You go to college or something?"

"A few semesters in the Pacific."

The door opened again and foul muggy air and a sallow-faced kid in work clothes came in. He wandered to the cigarette machine, put a quarter in, and pulled out his butts. He stood there fiddling with the pack until the bartender yelled, "*Hey!* Close that damn door!"

The kid said something dirty, finished opening the pack, lit a butt and walked out, leaving the bartender to go over and shut the damn door himself.

I said, "What's that smell?"

I'd noticed it before, but now it seemed worse than ever.

"Fish," she said, like she was tasting some that had gone off. "Tons of it. Also clams, crabs, and anything else that comes out of the ocean, all getting chopped, cooked and canned."

I shook my head. "Fish, my eye. If it is, that catch's been dead a long time."

She shook her head and the brunette hair bounced on her shoulders some more. "No, it's fish, all right. Until the war, it wasn't bad at all. But the factory took a contract to turn out glue and put up the new addition where they make it and *that's* what smells. Fish glue." She shuddered. "They say it makes more money than the cannery."

"Oh."

And so now I knew all about fish glue. Just plain glue, and the horses they made it from, wasn't bad enough. Now they made it out of fishes. Dead mackerel.

"I heard better fish stories," I said.

She shrugged. "It's the biggest industry in town. Senator Charles owns it." She took a long pull on the drink and set the glass down empty. "I used to work there, y'know. At the cannery. I had a pretty good job, too." Her hand made a wave at the room and herself. "That was before… this."

"What happened?"

"My boss had busy hands. I slapped him."

I grinned. "With a fish, I hope."

She grinned. "No. I had to make do with an ashtray."

"Well played," I said.

Another shrug, too small to make her hair dance. "One way to get fired."

The door opened again and more of the smell seeped in. Only this time it closed and stayed closed, after a wide, dish-faced blue-uniformed cop with a big belly held it open for a younger partner to come down the three steps from the street. They both looked around the room. You'd think there was something to see.

Everything got quiet awfully fast and one of the drunks at the bar turned around and lost his balance. He went flat on his face and the big cop stepped over him, barely noticing. The slick pair at the card table stopped playing and stared. *Were these two after them?*

I stared too because the big cop wasn't looking at the blackjack-playing pair but instead right at me, and the way he held that club meant he aimed to use it before asking any questions. He played it tough, the way nearly every stupid cop does, thinking that a uniform made him a superman and forgetting that other guys are just as big and maybe even tougher. With or without a billy.

He reached for me with one hand to hold on while he swung, and as soon as he had his fingers planted in my coat front, I pulled a nasty little trick that broke his arm above the elbow and he dropped to the floor screaming. The other cop was pulling his gun as he ran for me.

This one was stupid too. If I had gone the other way he would have had time to jerk the rod free, but I came in on him and split his face six ways to Sunday with a straight right and while he laid there, I put a foot on his belly and brought it down hard. Like I was stomping on a particularly ugly bug.

He turned blue for a while, then started breathing again.

The cop with the broken wing had fainted.

The bartender was wide-eyed over his open mouth.

Over in the corner, the slumming party looked sick to their stomachs, then got up and scrambled out.

The brunette hadn't reacted at all.

I said to the barkeep, "I'd like to know how goons like this pair got on the force."

There was a wheeze in the bartender's throat when

he told me. "For three hunnert bucks, you get put on the list." His eyes still seemed a little glassy. He looked at me, the phone on the wall, then toward the door, wondering what to do next.

"I don't know what the hell this is all about," I said, "but I don't like to get pushed. Not even a little bit."

He swallowed and nodded. No argument.

One of the drunks decided it was time for another drink and pounded on the bar to get it. I raked in my change, stuck the bills in my wallet and put the silver in my pocket.

The brunette smiled wistfully. "Another time, another place?"

"A better time," I said, "a better place."

I pulled out a ten and shoved it over to her. "Till then," I said. "Sorry to drink and run."

"Good luck," she said and smiled. She meant it too.

I had to step over the big-belly cop with the busted arm. I opened the door and stood sniffing the air. It stunk. Everything stunk about this burg.

But it went right with how I was feeling, so I didn't give a damn. I went up the few steps to the street, saw the empty squad car at the curb and got too damned cocky for my own good. Cops drive in pairs and I didn't expect any others to be hanging around.

But they were—they sure were.

Somebody yelled, "Cripes, there he goes!"

That was all I needed. I faded into the shadows alongside the building and took off as fast as I could. I skirted around the stone stoops, hurdled the boxes of rubbish packed against the railings and kept my head down all the way. The night started to scream with staccato blasts of gunfire while ricochets whistled off the pavement around me.

A slug tore into my shoe and knocked my foot out from under me. I hit the sidewalk on my tail, swearing my head off, wishing I had a rod in my hand that would tear the guts out of somebody—any "three-hunnert-dollar" cop would do.

Up ahead a street lamp doused the area and I knew if I went into that yellow splash of light, I'd be a dead duck. I couldn't go forward and I couldn't go back. I couldn't do a single damn thing except roll down the steps next to me until I hit a pile of newspapers and spilled them over on top of me.

I didn't get it. I didn't get it at all. I lay there with my lungs sucking air hungrily to stop the burning in my chest. *I come in undercover and suddenly I'm the main attraction.* My heart was slamming into my ribs and my mind was telling me to get the hell out of there in a goddamn hurry.

Sure, get out. Walk right up into a face full of bullets.

They were up there knowing right where I went and I could hear their feet converging on the spot. I pulled out the manila packet of green from under my coat, under my shirt, and tucked it in a gaping crack in the cement between the wall and the first step of the staircase that ran over my head. Tucked it in good, and hoped for the best, filling in with some pebbles. That left me with my wallet and a few bucks.

But I sure as hell didn't want to be found with that packet of green on me. The thirty-thousand dollars that brought me to Killington would wind up in the pockets of the bent cops who busted me.

Then I waited.

The door beside me that led to a cellar was too heavy to crash and the padlock too big to force. Go up and I'd die. Wait it out and maybe I wouldn't. So I stopped thinking and just waited.

A voice said, "*You down there!* Come out with your hands in the air."

"Why should I?"

"Would you sooner do it in a basket?"

I went up.

Slowly, my foot hurting a little, but the only things missing were the heel of my shoe and my damn dignity. I limped up the steps with my hands at shoulder level and stood on the landing looking at the hounds.

Ten of them altogether. One with a Tommy gun, for Christ's sake! Two with shotguns. One with a sack brimming with gas bombs. Suddenly I was the Capone mob crossed with the James Gang. The others were practically unarmed except for little bitty snub-nosed revolvers that held tiny tickets to hell.

For that much I was grateful. Another inch on the barrels of those things and I would have got it in the back when I was running.

A tall, cadaverous, derby-sporting guy in plainclothes with a shotgun and a sneer nodded and the rest formed a semicircle around me, like I was a quarterback who wandered into the wrong huddle. Windows were opening all over the place and the heads that poked out were screaming questions across the street that weren't being answered. Maybe these windows and the faces in them would keep me alive long enough to find out what made me worth rounding up.

And maybe killing.

When I had gotten frisked from my hat to my shoes, one of them said, "He's clean."

"Try again and be sure."

Hands patted me down again. "Nothing."

Finally I'd had about as much of it as I could take.

"Somebody's going to do a lot of explaining, chums," I said, my words bland but the edge in my voice something that could cut you.

The back of a hand rocked my head and dumped me right on my ass. The same guy hauled me up and was going to try it again, only a flashbulb popped and blinded the both of us.

All I could see were twin bright spots of brilliant white, but I could hear the cops arguing with the photographer, who got the best of it without half trying. Apparently Freedom of the Press had gotten around even in Killington.

Somebody said, "Hell, let him *have* his damn picture. He can get plenty more later, too."

A couple more bulbs went off while the boys were crowding in around me. I got shoved into the back of a car as a uniformed cop came puffing up, yelling, "Y'oughta see what he did to Jenkins and Wilby! Ya oughta *see* it! Get an ambulance down there fast. *Cripes!*"

"What'd he do?" the photog asked. "Who is this guy? I thought Dillinger was dead."

"Come on, Lieutenant Sykes," another voice called, apparently the reporter who traveled with the camera guy. "This is for publication. What's the damn *story*?"

The tall plainclothes dick in the derby was in the front seat of the unmarked car now. He leaned out the window, his shotgun in his lap.

"You'll get it later," he said. This was Sykes, apparently. To his driver and all the cops surrounding, he called, "*Roll those cars!*"

Now the reporter leaned in, ignoring that. "We'll get it *now*. What's he bein' held for?"

"Sex murderer. He raped and killed a factory worker named Jean Warburton a couple hours ago. We got him cold."

Which was how the muggy night suddenly got.
Cold.

CHAPTER TWO

The lights damn near burned the raw skin off my face. They ate into my eyes until everything was blurred, and when I went to wipe my vision clear, a hand with a wet leather glove on it would push my fingers away. My lips were swollen tight around my teeth, with my tongue a dry rough rasp that licked ineffectually at my mouth.

There would be a question followed by a smack, the sound of it wet. Fingers would try to twist the ears off my head and the flat of a palm would snap against the back of my neck until there wasn't any feeling left in me at all.

I was in a small room with no furniture but the hard chair I'd been slammed into. My right hand was cuffed to a uniformed cop standing beside me. A lamp with the kind of wattage you can get a sunburn from was craning its neck at me curiously, like some weird damn bird. The room had enough floating rank cigar smoke to please a bunch of backroom politicians.

The tall dick called Sykes wasn't just supervising—he liked to get involved. I could make him out all right, but his bully boys were just more of the blur. Between slaps and questions and answers I gave that nobody cared about, he would lean in and train light-blue eyes on me that were oh so pretty, in a long angular puss that wasn't pretty at all.

Sykes leaned back out of the light and said, "We'll go through it again. Your name is Mike Hammer."

I nodded, wishing I could work up enough spit to spatter all over his shoes.

"You're a bum," the tall detective said clinically.

I shrugged. "You're a bastard."

The wet leather glove had a fist in it that splatted against my cheek—Sykes doing his own hitting.

"You got off a freight in the yards," Sykes said, "picked up this tomato and killed her. Don't try to lie your way out of it."

I searched for just the right words and used them. The fist came into the light and did the same thing again. I said the words again. This went on for a while.

A door creaked open. Heavy footsteps came in.

A rough-edged voice outside the light cut in with, "Pretty tough, huh?"

Sykes again: "We'll soften him up."

"Better leave it go for a while. He's marked up enough as it is."

The sarcasm came out of Sykes all sing-songy: "Maybe we should give him a big feed and a soft bed. Maybe we ought to get him a nice friendly broad to sleep with, too, keep him warm and happy."

"Henny," the rough voice answered, with tired exasperation, "do as you're told for a change. Softening him up some is one thing. Outright beatings I don't put up with—how many times do I…?" A long sigh. "Bring him up to my office."

I couldn't make it on my own steam, so they half-carried me. Most of the lights were off this time of night at City Hall or anyway the police station part. They dragged me through shadows while footsteps on the finished concrete floor echoed in the hall like erratic gunfire. Muffled traffic sounds said the world was still out there somewhere. Nice to know.

We went up a few steps to a corridor, got in an elevator until it wheezed up and whined to a stop, then went down another shadowy corridor to an office with HERMAN BELDEN, CHIEF OF POLICE lettered on the frosted glass of the door. This was a good-size office with a green-shaded lamp on a big oak desk with awards and citations on the wall and a thick rug on the floor with decent furniture here and there. I got my eyes open long enough to take all that in before they closed again.

The chair they threw me in wasn't like the one downstairs. This one was big and soft with smooth arms and leather upholstery that took some of the ache out. There were no lights that burned and no smell of cheap cigars here. I'd been hauled back into civilization. The rough-edged voice rattled off a couple of names and told them to stay. The rest went outside.

Somebody ran water from a cooler into a cup and threw the works in my face. It was the nicest thing they could have done for me. The splash washed out my eyes so they could open most of the way and took some of the stiffness from my mouth. The cup came back again, this time to my lips, and I went for it until there was none left.

I sat there for a good minute before anybody said anything. My host, Herman Belden, was the stocky, middle-aged guy in the swivel chair behind the desk, all thinning hair, pouchy eyes, thick lips, and mottled skin. His purple tie was loose and he was in shirtsleeves with sweat circles under his arms. Tall Henny Sykes, in a brown suit and darker brown tie, derby in hand, looked like he never broke a sweat in his life. He glowered at me from his position by the door, arms folded, legs crossed though he was standing up. Another big detective stood right beside me, a couple hundreds of pounds of potatoes in a cheap suit, swinging a leather-covered billy into the palm of his hand like a cop walking his beat.

Only right now *I* was his beat.

In the corner, in a white blouse, black skirt, and low black heels, a female hardcase with a decent build chewed gum while she doodled on her steno pad. Taking notes during the Third Degree was nothing new to her. Behind the hornrim glasses and under the piled-up dishwater hair, she had features that could stand up to dim lighting, but five would get you ten, if you screwed her, she'd be chewing gum then, too.

Belden put down the sheet he was staring at and picked up something else. My wallet. He thumbed out two tens and a couple of ones, laid a few cards down beside each other and arranged them into various positions. The dockworkers union card was there, Social Security, driver's license. Satisfied with his arrangement his eyes crawled up to mine.

He rose and wandered over, as if he just noticed someone was in his office, his voice polite with a sandpaper finish. "Shall we talk now, Mr. Hammer?"

My grin was a fake, but it made me feel better. "Nuts. Either you book me or let me out of here. If I'm booked, I get a phone call."

A grunt made his belly shake, like the kind of department store Santa that sent kids screaming. "Know a lot about the legal system, do you, son?"

"That much I do."

His smile had a puckish quality, as if he enjoyed a little light banter between dishing out beatings. "In this state we can hold you seventy-two hours without doing a damn thing. How do you like that?"

"I got nothing pressing."

His mouth tightened. "Then we have plenty of time to talk."

"Go ahead and talk," I said. "I'd like to know what this is all about myself."

Any goodwill left in his face disappeared altogether. "I don't know why you people insist on doing it this way, but since I'm more or less legally obliged to explain the crime even to the criminal himself, I'll give you a run-through."

You people? Freight-car riding bums? Strangers hauled in and beaten senseless? Citizens in general whose very existence was an annoyance to hardworking public officials?

"At eleven fifteen," Belden was saying, pacing slowly before me like a D.A. summing up for a jury, "a white male approximately thirty years of age was seen to accost a young woman on South Richmond Street. There appeared to be an argument about the pick-up, and the male dragged the woman off into the bushes. The witness managed to get close enough to see pants around the now-prone male's ankles, and to hear the victim's screams. The witness ran for the police, but when they returned, the woman had been killed by strangulation and obviously raped, and the male was no longer around. The search started and you were picked up. You were positively identified by the witness who saw you accost the woman. Is there anything else you'd like to know?"

"Yeah. When do I get to see this witness?"

Belden made a vague motion. "Bring him," he told Sykes.

The tall plainclothes cop opened the door, said something to somebody outside, then maybe a minute passed before a skinny little guy in a filthy rumpled suit was ushered in by an arm. He needed a shave as badly as I did, and stood wringing his battered hat in his hands and finally stuffed it in a frayed pocket. His eyes went around the room until they found me, opened a little wider as he licked his lips, then went back to Sykes, who nodded just enough to identify me to this ringer.

The chief said, "This the man?"

"That's him all right." He bobbed his head and tried to find some place to put his hands, his watery eyes landing everywhere except on the guy he was fingering.

"Okay?" Sykes asked Belden.

Belden had a world-weariness as he said, "Okay."

Sykes tapped the witness on the shoulder, got a startled look, then led him back outside again.

Belden returned to his desk and his swivel chair, and put on his phony good-natured smile. "Well, Mr. Hammer?"

"I'm impressed. You got most of the liquor smell off him."

"What are you insinuating?"

"I'm 'insinuating' he's full of crap," I said. I made something of a show of not being impressed. "I don't know why he's lying, but I'll tell you, flat out—I was eating supper when this sex kill was supposed to have happened."

A disgusted sigh made Belden's heavy body move in the chair, as if a hedgehog were burrowing just under ground. "Where?"

"A hash house near the yards. It had a signal switch for a sign outside the door."

Belden and Sykes exchanging glances said they knew the place. The chief picked up a pencil and tapped it on the desk. "Think anybody there could identify you?"

I leaned back in the chair with my breath feeling a little less strained in my throat. The remains of a butt and some matches were in my pocket. They let me light the thing, which was more than they did downstairs.

"Sure," I said. "The waitress who took my order. We had a nice talk for a few minutes. She got a buck tip out of me. She'll remember."

"For your sake, Hammer," the chief said, "I hope she does."

But somehow I didn't think he hoped that at all.

This time the joint was nearly empty.

It was between shifts at the yards and, during the break, most of the help was in back, cleaning up. Lonnie Shaker was the owner's name, a bald little guy with an Italian accent, who shook hands with the chief, grinning too big and too much, then squeezed out a nod for Sykes and the two sour-eyed detectives with him.

Belden nodded toward the kitchen. "You got the same bunch working now that was on around eleven?"

"Yeah, sure." Lonnie waved his thumb behind him. "They in there. What's up?"

"We need an identification. Tell him, Hammer."

I said to the manager, "A blonde waitress with dark streaks in her hair. Prettiest one working, when I was here. Green eyes?"

"Oh sure." A smile crinkled Lonnie's mouth. "That's Louise." His butter-wouldn't-melt smile went to Belden. "You wait. I'll get her for you."

He went back through the swinging doors and his voice got lost in the clatter of crockery. The cop I was with pulled out a pack of butts, stuck one in his mouth, remembered I was there too, and handed the pack over.

I nodded thanks and got myself a smoke out, my hand shaking.

For a minute my trembling hand guiding the cigarette to my lips was the only thing in the room that moved—a big, palsied paw, doing a shimmy that held every eye fixed. The dick I was cuffed to gave me a light, waved out the match. Not a bad guy, I thought. Then I noticed his nasty, knowing smile.

The chill started at my scalp and crept all the way down into my shoes, like cold water on the verge of turning to ice. When I looked up, I could see their faces. Henny Sykes sneering as he sat casually on the edge of a nearby table; the dick on my right nodding; Belden rocking back on his heels—a cop chorus singing a wordless song that said it was all over but the hanging.

Or the frying.

What I had left of my guts started turning to mush. *This damned thing was a nightmare!* The lousy bastards were putting the screws on me and getting ready to turn them tighter.

I felt like screaming but couldn't get a sound out. The cigarette fell from my fingers as the waitress came through the door and, seeing her blank expression, I could feel the clamps come down hard and cold. It was coming, I knew it was, but there wasn't a goddamn thing I could do about it.

The dame was looking at us and her eyes passed right over mine, like I wasn't there at all, a stone skipping across a pond. Those eyes were a lovely green, all right. Lovely, green, and empty.

Belden said, "You were on all evening, miss?"

She nodded once. Her forehead puckered up between her eyes, like that was a tough question and she really had to concentrate. "That's right. Haven't been off the floor, except to go in the kitchen."

"Do you remember tonight's customers?"

"Oh sure. I know most of them by name."

"You'd remember anybody new?"

Two nods this time. "Practically everybody that comes in here are regulars. Anybody new would stand out."

Belden's head came around to me slowly. He said, "Ever see this man before?"

Nothing showed in her face. She was looking right at me and nothing.

"I was here from eleven to eleven thirty," I prompted.

She cocked her head as if trying to find something, anything, familiar about me.

And I was puffy and scuffed up, so maybe…

"Damn it," I said, "these punks messed me up, but look close—you'll remember me. We talked about New York. I sat over there at the counter and gave you a buck tip."

But I was talking to myself.

She drew back from me, white rubbing out the flush in her cheeks. "I, uh…" Her empty gaze returned to Belden. "He wasn't in here. Sorry. No."

I leaned forward, held back by the dick. "Damnit, girl, *think*, will you? I sat right over there! We talked! You *must* re—"

The girl was shaking her head, still looking right at the bulky Belden.

He said, "Okay miss, thanks for your cooperation. We'll get a statement from you later."

She got back behind the counter.

The dick yanked on the handcuff. "Come on, you."

My sneering disgust took all the Cossacks in. "You stinking crooked bastards, you lousy, scrimy—"

Sykes didn't bother with gloves this time, he just came off the edge of the table and the knuckles of his right fist smashed my nose into a bloody pulp. His face was livid with rage and he was getting set to try it again, hard bony fists ready. I half leaned against the cop beside me feeling the blood drip off my chin.

Belden's voice held a flat snarl. "*Jesus!* Sykes, this time it goes on your record, and enough of this could damn well cost you your badge. Maybe you'll learn to act on *orders* someday."

I watched Sykes get madder, watched his lips thin out into a pale gash of rage, heard him say, "Yes, sir," as sarcastically as he could.

But it was more than he could take. His mind was saying the hell with Belden and he stepped in to take another shot at me and soon as he took that one step forward, I kicked him in the crotch so hard, he lifted off the floor, his pants ripping, and the next second he was a screaming, gasping lump on the floor, doubled up into a knot. His mouth was coughing up a bloody, foaming vomit. He didn't even look human.

The little waitress took this in with terror, a hand curled at her cheek. I hoped she was the one who had to clean up that puke.

My arm was twisted up behind my neck, and if it wasn't for Belden, the dick at my side would have torn it off. Two uniformed guys came in at Belden's call and carried Sykes out like a guy who took a really bad hit on the football field. They dragged him out to the car and pushed me in the other one.

Now I felt better.

Pushing back always made me feel better.

I was in the back seat, grinning to myself. A uniformed cop was driving and Belden was riding. He glanced over a shoulder at me.

"Sykes is a bad enemy to make, son," he told me, shaking his head. Such concern.

The driver asked, "Back to the station, Chief?"

"No," Belden said. "Make it the morgue."

The hospital was in the middle of town, surrounded by housing that were more like hovels. It was an ancient brick structure that had the kind of gothic look Dr. Frankenstein might have gone for, lacking only lightning in the background to really set it off. Getting hauled to this nightmarish joint for medical attention would be bad enough.

But the morgue was in the basement.

Somewhere water dripped, as an antiseptic smell did battle with a general musty dankness. The corridor walls were concrete block, the floor just plain concrete. Leaving the other cops behind, Belden took me by the arm through double doors into a high-ceilinged, chilly area where half a dozen sheet-covered corpse-accommodating wheeled trays were waiting to move their passengers to refrigerated drawers lining the walls nearby.

The attendant was a gray little man: gray hair, gray eyes, gray skin, gray suit glimpsed under a white smock with irregular maroon dried-blood striping. He had a lidded-eyed look that seemed like boredom at first but was really the deadness that he had caught, like the flu, from his tenants.

"Warburton girl," Belden told him.

The gray attendant checked his clipboard. "No autopsy yet," he said.

"We want a quick look at her."

Someone came in behind us.

As we turned, Belden told me in a helpful whisper, "Medical examiner."

The M.E. was small and plump, his suit a three-piece tweed not appropriate to this time of year, unless you spent a lot of time in a room as cold as this. He had a round face, thinning white hair, and a tiny smile that was strictly a superficial wound.

"Dr. Helton," Belden said. "What can you tell us?"

Helton frowned at me. "Who's this?"

"Our suspect," the chief said.

At least he hadn't said "killer."

The M.E. said, "Hold out your hands, son."

I said, "Why?"

"Just do it," Belden said.

"Do you have lawyers in this town?" I asked. "Because I'm thinking I could use one. Like to advise me to tell you two to shove it."

Belden gave me a look that said the small amount of goodwill he'd displayed was about to vanish. "Your *hands*, Hammer."

I showed the little doc my hands. He just looked, didn't touch.

"About right," he said.

"For what?" I asked.

"Large and powerful enough," the M.E. said, "to have strangled that young woman."

"I didn't strangle anybody!"

The M.E. shrugged. "That's between you and your God. And the courts."

Belden asked, "But can you confirm she was raped?"

The pudgy little M.E. shrugged one shoulder. "The police report includes ripped garments, her panties being torn off her and tossed aside. There was semen in her vagina. Definitely sexual intercourse took place shortly before her death. In the circumstances, there's little likelihood it was consensual."

I said to Belden, "Did you two rehearse this before or after your dress rehearsal with that little waitress?"

Belden gave me a cold look. "Maybe you'd like me to turn Sykes loose on you again? Really have him take off the gloves."

"He likes working with his gloves on," I reminded him.

Belden said to the M.E., "Give us a look at her."

The M.E. followed the gray little man to a nearby tray and let his associate do the flipping back of the sheet.

She was naked and, even in death, beautiful, in the way a cold marble statue can be beautiful. The bruising on her throat where strong hands had gripped stood out like dark filthy streaks on the alabaster skin. When a mortician got through with her, everybody would say it looked like she was only sleeping. Right now she was just tragedy on a morgue tray.

I must have been staring, because Belden said, "Admiring your handiwork, Hammer? Or are you gonna claim you never saw her before."

"Never talked to her in my life," I said.

Which was true.

But I had seen her. I wasn't about to tell Belden, but I'd seen her all right.

In the window of a sleeper car.

CHAPTER THREE

They called it a coroner's jury.

Tight faces and horrified expressions. An energetic little District Attorney determined to see immediate justice done. Cops with their knowing eyes at the doors and windows. That same hardcase stenog still chewing gum, and reporters anxious to get it all down on paper. An audience with glittering, sadistic eyes watching the rape-killer.

On the table in front of me was a newspaper, the *Killington Morning Herald*, with all the facts, if you could call them that. Mostly it was an account of the vicious fight I had put up and the heroism of the police. It ended on a sad note. Captain Henry "Henny" Sykes, winner of so many police department commendations, was hospitalized after a cowardly attack by the suspect. Critical condition, it said. Maybe my kick in the balls meant fatherhood for Henny would in future be a moot point. Maybe his voice would change back again and he could stop shaving too.

The picture of me was a good likeness, anyway. It had been taken at my arrest, before Sykes and company turned my face into a puffy balloon. Right now the swelling had gone down, but the various bruises and scrapes made me look like I hadn't washed in a while. The cheap suit they'd provided for this court appearance reeked of mothballs.

A gavel rapped and the coroner called the assembly to order. When things quieted down, he looked at me, frowned and asked, "Are you sure you do not want to be represented by an attorney?"

"I don't know any kangaroos," I said.

Somebody in the audience caught on and snickered. The coroner gaveled the chamber to order and gave me a frown like the one my old man would give me before the razor strop came out.

Hell, why bore you with the details.

The pint-size D.A. got up, smoothed his perfect, perfectly expensive dark suit, and went through the routine point by point. He painted a picture of me as a bum who hopped off a freight in the railroad yards, committed the most heinous crime there was, and who was about to do the same to another woman in a barroom when he was picked up. He went through all the motions, all the words plain and fancy, and by the time he got finished telling about the two cops in the bar and Henny Sykes at the hash house, he didn't need to bring on any witnesses at all.

But as a formality, he trotted out the alky runt and had him wave a shaking finger in my direction and tell all the gruesome details over again: girl dragged in the bushes, pants around the ankles, the sordid works.

When he finished questioning the so-called witness, the coroner turned to me where I sat at a table with a cop cuffed to my wrist, and asked patronizingly, "Would you like to cross-examine the witness?"

I shook my head. "No thanks."

For that I got another frown. The D.A. wound things up with some blow-ups of the dead girl at the crime scene, which he passed around to the jury and got a few of them sick to their stomachs. The dead babe didn't look a bit pretty with her eyes bugging out like that, but the flashes of nudity provided a tawdry bit of relief for the creeps in the crowd.

When he finished, the jury marched out, marched back in, and said there was sufficient evidence to hold me over for the grand jury.

I'd have said the same, if I hadn't been on the wrong end of it.

At ten minutes past two, they trooped me into the District Attorney's courthouse office, a big high-ceilinged affair with a conference table at one end and the kind of furniture the taxpayers had no idea they could afford.

At the other end of the office, in front of a mahogany desk the size of the ice floe that took the *Titanic* down, Chief Belden was waiting, wearing his latest rumpled bed of a suit and a put-upon expression. With all that mottled flesh on that thick-lipped, pouchy-eyed puss, he looked like a guy trying to figure out what disease he was dying of.

Belden waved to a chair he had ready and pulled one up himself. To the D.A., he said, "You shoulda come down to my office. I have more to do than drive this guy all over town, you know."

The D.A. got behind his desk, the size of it making him look even smaller than he was. His hair had that black patent leather George Raft look, and his chin was sharp enough to stick his memos on. He sat, then shoved a fancy wooden box of cigars across his desk.

"Have one, Herman, and relax, why don't you?"

Belden shifted in his chair and reached for a corona. They didn't offer me one, for some reason, or my cop escort, either.

"Now, Mr. Hammer," the D.A. said, leaning back in his chair, "I suppose you know the seriousness of the charge against you?"

"He knows, all right," Belden muttered through his cigar smoke. "He knows too damn *much* if you ask me."

The D.A.'s response to the chief was clipped: "I'm not asking *you*."

Belden shrugged.

"So what if I know?" I said. "What about it?"

"You heard the verdict of the coroner's jury."

"Yeah, they got me so worried I'm ready to confess and cop a manslaughter plea. Right after I bust out crying."

Belden said, "See?"

The D.A. simpered, hating to let himself smile. "You seem familiar with court practice and procedure, Mr. Hammer."

That answered one question: they hadn't traced me back to Manhattan and my private investigator's license. Somehow I didn't think they were trying very hard.

"I got a C-plus in Civics," I said.

The little D.A. smiled in a way that suggested he was tasting it. "Then you should realize just how hopeless your case is."

"Don't embarrass yourself," I said.

His eyes and nostrils flared. "Excuse me?"

"You don't seem like a complete jerk," I said. "You really want to see your little witness on the stand? You really want to see what a good lawyer will do to him? That guy never saw me haul that dame into the bushes any more than he laid eyes on you doing it. I'm going to relish the nice stink that'll rise over the way the cops in this town treat a citizen. I can't wait to see what the New York City papers do to your hides when this thing comes to court."

"What you'll see, Hammer," he told me, unimpressed, "is how much sympathy a sexual psychopath gets." There was ice in his voice. "I'm giving you a chance to confess this thing and make it easier on yourself, but if you don't want to cooperate… then that's your affair. You can yell police brutality all you want, but I don't think it will make much difference to a jury. Rape murderers aren't generally treated with kid gloves."

"You forget something."

"Do I?"

"You've had these papers you got in your pocket splash all kinds of lies around about me. You've set me up as a monster who would have made Hitler sick to his stomach. So how do you turn around and give me some lesser charge, and get away with it with the public?"

He shifted in his chair a little. "That's our worry."

"Shit."

"Watch your mouth, Hammer," Belden said. He drew in on his corona and made a face into the smoke as he looked at the D.A. "When's the trial coming up?"

The slick little prosecutor flipped a hand. "As soon as it can be arranged."

Belden gave me a sideways nod. "He's right about the papers."

"Exactly. That's why this case has been pushed ahead."

I leaned back in my chair. "Quick justice."

The D.A. bobbed his head slowly. "But fair. You'll be extended every chance."

"Thanks. But don't think for a second you're going to get away with assigning me some local shyster."

He flipped the other hand. "We of course would provide someone, and some of the top attorneys in the area do pro bono work. But if you want representation from out of town, we'll help you arrange that. Assuming you can afford the… the freight, shall we say?"

"You're too good to me. For a frame, this stinks. It's not even a good fit."

Belden's cigar came away from his mouth slowly. "Man, I told you to watch your mouth." A tic pulled his lips apart momentarily. "Anybody who says I'm out to frame a guy is asking for it. Say that stuff in a court, you better be able to prove it. Say it to my face and take your goddamn chances, boy."

I grinned at him. "Want me to say it again?"

The tic was more noticeable this time. "Yeah. Say it." He rested the cigar on a tray on the desk. He formed ham-size fists just waiting to club me.

I said it.

For a minute I thought I'd had it. His shoulder came back ready to bring the sledge around. The D.A. cleared his throat and Belden glanced his way. Winced. Sighed.

Then he relaxed. Gave me a sick smile. "Okay, Hammer, it's your show. Tell me about it. Chapter and verse. I'm all ears."

I eased my legs out. "I've been doing that. Nobody seems interested. If you're on the level, Chief, what will it take? How about getting me a polygraph? You have heard of lie detectors?"

The D.A. frowned. "That isn't admissible as evidence."

Belden, though, was interested. Maybe he wasn't in on the frame after all; maybe it had just been delivered to him with a big red bow.

He said, "You pass it, and it'll influence police action just the same. You asking for that, Hammer?"

"I am. And what have you got to lose, trying it out on me?"

Killers don't ask for lie detector tests and guys trying to lay a frame don't agree to it. But these two did. They sure did, nodding at each other and me immediately. The D.A. looked almost pleased about it. Could he be clean in this, too?

Belden said to the D.A., "Want me to call for the gimmick?"

"The Providence police will cooperate," the prosecutor said. "They'll send their own operator too." I got another nice smile from the D.A. "An unbiased operator will certainly forestall a lot of nonsense in the press. And if he passes…" He turned back to Belden and rocked in his swivel chair. "How long will it take?"

The chief, wreathed in cigar smoke, shrugged. "A week maybe."

"Fine. Perhaps by that time the defendant here will take the opportunity to consider his options."

"Why not?" I said.

They looked at me without any expression at all.

"And when I beat this rap," I said, "maybe I'll stick around and see what the hell it was all about in the first place. And meet a few guys away from the station who like to use wet gloves when they work a guy over. It ought to be fun."

Belden's upper lip curled back over his teeth. "Fun is right, mister. But if you don't beat the rap, you suppose you'll die laughing?"

It didn't take a week.

It took two days for the lie-test expert to arrive, and by that time I had been crucified but good in the local papers. The out-of-town editions of the New York sheets didn't even bother to carry the story, but I was quite a sensation here in the old home town. Garden clubs rose in demanding more police protection for young females, political associations promised to see fast action, and the columnists were sounding off about how I'd cooked my own goose, demanding a lie detector test. I was buried before they even killed me.

The double guard around my cell block was relieved for supper and, five minutes later, Belden came around to gather me for the test. He had a pair of uniformed cops along, swinging billies.

"Be nice, Hammer," he advised, giving me a lot more teeth than that phony a smile required.

I didn't have to be told. Making a break for it was out of the question. Behind me those billy boys were waiting. Anxiously waiting. The lad who swung one widest was the fat boy from the bar, his other arm in a cast. Maybe I should offer to sign it for him.

They had the machine set up in Belden's office. The operator was a middle-aged guy with steel-gray hair and steel-rimmed glasses who didn't bother to look up when I came in. Why bother? He'd already seen it all.

He dropped a dead cigarette to the floor while I sat down in that same comfortable chair as before, then adjusted the arm band and the sweat pads and fiddled around until he was sure everything was set. He nodded once to Belden.

One of the cops walked to the door, opened it and called out, "All set, sir."

He held the door open and the D.A. came in with the wolf pack at his heels. All of them: promising young assistants, butt-kissing lower echelon with their steno pads, two boys who looked at each other with pursed-kiss lips over their briefcases, and the hardcase female who was still working her gum. I wondered if it was the same damn piece.

The other four were reporters. Two had cameras and copped a couple of quickies of me propped in the chair tied down to the machine. Jackson of the *Herald*, "How does the gizmo work, doc?"

A fresh cigarette in the operator's mouth hardly moved as he said, "The name is Lewis Hanson, young man. I am not a doctor."

"Sorry, Mr. Hanson. Care to make a statement? This is the first time one of these gadgets has been used here."

I grinned at him. "Go on, explain."

"Briefly, it's quite simple," he told the reporter. "It takes more effort to lie than to tell the truth. When a greater effort is made, the body speeds up. Slight as the effort is, the machine can detect it. There's a difference in pulse rate, amount of perspiration and so on."

"Just like that," Jackson said, his smile mildly skeptical. "Foolproof."

Hanson shot him a disgusted look. "Far from it. For that reason many states will not accept results as evidence." His head came around slowly and he stared at me. "Extreme nervousness, for example, can influence results."

I grinned again. "Nuts. I'm feeling great."

The reporter took that down too.

Hell, what did I have to worry about?

It took ten minutes for everybody to get set. They parked in chairs behind me and shuffled their feet on the floor, dancing in place. The place got smoky so Belden opened the window. That made it worse. The stink from the fish factory crawled in on the night air until I told him to shut the damned thing and be satisfied with the smoke. The window slid back in place.

Then they got on with the show. The script was a sheaf of papers in Hanson's hand.

"Your name?"

"Mike Hammer."

"Age?"

"Twenty-seven."

"Occupation?"

"Self-employed."

"What kind of work?"

"Various jobs."

"Are you married?"

"No."

"Engaged?"

"No."

"Do women interest you?"

"Naturally."

Somebody snickered and a muted voice said to shut up. The questions rolled on and came back again. Repeats. Double checks. What year was I born. When was I last in bed with a woman. This. That. And the next thing.

Next page of the script.

Had I ever killed anybody? And when he said that, everybody leaned forward. I said dozens and meant it and told them I had the medals to prove it.

Hanson nodded solemnly. "Mr. Hammer," he said, "now I am going to ask you a series of yes-or-no questions. Please restrict these answers to yes or no. Do not explicate."

"All right."

He gave me the date in question, then asked, "Did you arrive in Killington on that evening?"

"Yes."

"Did you arrive at approximately ten-forty-five p.m.?"

"Yes."

"Did you travel by train?"

"Yes."

"Did you have a ticket on that train?"

"No."

"Did you hop a freight?"

"Yes."

"Did you approach a young woman on South Richmond Street at around eleven-fifteen p.m.?"

"No."

"Did you rape a young woman the evening in question?"

"No."

"Did you strangle a young woman to death the evening in question?"

"No."

"Did you eat eggs and bacon at the Switchhouse Diner around eleven-fifteen p.m. the evening in question?"

"Yes."

He asked again and again. I said no to rape and strangulation and yes to bacon and eggs. More questions and he came back to *the* questions again and I still said no twice and yes once. The last page of the script went by and all my answers were the same as far as I knew and the show was over.

Belden gave me a cigarette and lit it while Hanson detached me from the gimmick.

The *Herald* reporter grabbed another shot, folded his camera back into its case and said, "How'd it go, Doc? Did he do the deed or not?"

"Clear the room please," Hanson said.

I finished my cigarette, doused it in an ashtray on the desk, then stood. Herman Belden took my elbow and waved to the door with his thumb. "Now that the bedtime story's over, Hammer, it's time for beddie-bye."

So we marched back up the echoey corridors and down past the rows of cells until we came to the special job with the electric lock, and before the door was even opened all the way, the butt end of a nightstick rammed into my kidneys so hard my bladder let go as I headed toward the floor.

Behind me the big belly cop said, "Tough guy."

The lock clicked first, then Belden's voice rasped, "That'll cost you, Sarge! You know I don't go for that crap."

"It's worth it," the cop told him.

I got off my hands and knees and sat down on the floor, my groin sopping. The three of them were looking at me through the bars like monkeys.

"Have your secretary send me a carbon of the report in the morning, Chief," I managed. "If I like it, tell her I'll buy her a fresh stick of gum."

Belden's face froze. "I won't wait, wise guy. I'll bring it to you myself. I want to see your face change shape when you get the bad news. Maybe you'll even cry."

I was already close to that.

When they left I did what I had to. I staggered over to the sink and puked up my supper. I couldn't put my hand over my kidneys without feeling the pain wrench at my insides, so I stood there cursing between retchings until there was nothing to cough up except something bitter that made me sicker than ever. I managed to let go of the sink and trudge to the cot where I took off my wet trousers and flopped belly down on the ticking with my face buried in my arms.

I didn't get it. I didn't get it at all. *Why had I been fingered for this crap?* But sure as shit *somebody* was going to get it when I went out those front doors to the open air again. One hell of a lot of people were going to get taken apart piece by piece, and it would be a long time before the good people of Killington put the finger on a guy without asking questions first.

I lay there with my eyes closed until I was asleep. I didn't dream. I never dream, or anyway I never remember if I do. I knew I was asleep when the fire in my kidney went out and I knew I was awake when somebody lit it again.

Belden stood over me like a colossus with a book of judgment in his hand. The world outside the little high barred window was still dark—if this was morning, dawn hadn't come yet.

When he saw my head move, Belden said, "I brought the report, Hammer."

I started to turn over. "Now you know."

I got my feet on the floor.

He shook his head and I saw his teeth flash in the semi-darkness. "Now we *don't* know. The polygraph didn't prove a thing. The results were inconclusive."

My voice sounded weak. Almost gone. "You're lying!"

He tapped the sheets in his hand. "No. It's all here. Nothing definite could be established except your age maybe. As far as you're concerned, it's as damning as a negative report. You'll get the benefit of the doubt from the D.A. and he'll stick to the evidence at hand. Want to read it?"

"Get the hell out of here," I said.

"Sure, whatever you want. You can go back to sleep now. Maybe you'll think of that poor girl you killed. You know, I'm going to be there when the state cuts you loose from living. I'm going to enjoy it, in fact. One thing I always wanted to get my hands on, in this line of work, and that was a goddamned sex killer."

"Get the hell out!" I said again. The sweat on me turned cold. It even put out the fire in my back.

Belden grinned and tossed the report down on the cot. "Too bad you don't have a bedside lamp. You could look for loopholes." The lock on the door clicked and he stood on the other side of the bars, watching me in the pale glow of the overhead light.

"I'll tell you something, Hammer. For a while there I thought you weren't kidding about that frame. When you asked for a polygraph test, I started to get ideas about somebody having it in for you. You sure are one cocky bastard."

A laugh rattled in his throat as he walked away. I picked up the report and threw it across the room.

I had been too smart by half. I had requested the lie test and screwed myself over, because while I had told the truth in every instance, I knew down underneath that I was being evasive. The real reason I was here, and even who exactly I was, I'd kept hidden. And revealing it now would put everything at risk.

Nothing to do but ride it out.

Ride it out, and curse these damn sons of bitches and their billy clubs and wet gloves.

CHAPTER FOUR

It was morning.

Not a very pretty morning, because the sun was behind a blanket of rain that beat down hard enough to stir up the fish stink and drive it in through the concrete walls. I wondered if the people who lived and worked in this town got so used to the stench, if it didn't even register anymore.

What smell? they might ask.

But the fishy smell in Killington went way beyond the cannery and its glue factory cousin. It permeated whatever powers had put the finger on me and spread enough money and/or influence to make various citizens get up on their hind legs and lie to put me in the jail wing of the police station, with a transfer to Sing Sing and Old Sparky waiting in the wings.

As the expressly selected patsy, I was special enough

to get served breakfast in my cell. I found out why when they marched the other joes through to the mess hall. They were a lousy bunch of pimps, muggers, thieves, and killers, but they were all better than a fiend like me.

So much better that Belden—who maybe harbored some faint qualm that I might be telling the truth—was scared they might try something fancy on me, like a carving job with a water glass, because they found a sex killer's company too hard to take.

Anyway, I ate alone.

Later a cop with a gun on his hip—not a guard, because they went unarmed—came by and asked me if I wanted to exercise. Not eager to go anywhere alone with any of these bastards, particularly one packing, I told him to shove it. He studied me from his side of the bars, maybe wondering if he should give me a private consultation. But there were enough prisoners and real guards around to make that risky, even in this burg.

At ten o'clock the town chimes went through their routine and, as they finished, the cop came back again, gave me a sour look, opened the door and let in the diminutive D.A. with the expensive threads and the patent-leather hair.

"Mr. Hammer," he said, with butter-wouldn't-melt concern, "you really do need to arrange representation."

I was sitting on my edge of the cot, which let the shrimp tower over me.

I said, "Then give me a long-distance call. I don't want any of your local so-called legal talent."

He gave me a long-suffering sigh. "You have a right to make a call, Mr. Hammer, but not a long-distance one. What we're offering is *not* standard public defender office counsel. I've spoken personally, individually, to the four best criminal defense lawyers in town."

"And whose pocket are they in?"

His mouth tightened and his face went pale. "What the hell is wrong with you, man? You must know what you're facing. Let me help you. I have no desire to see you get…"

He looked for the word, but I gave it to him before he found it: "Railroaded?"

The pale face got suddenly red in its cheeks. "I just want to help you get proper representation."

That rated half a smile. "Let me tell you why, since I'm skeptical when the guy prosecuting me for rape and murder wants to 'help.' You don't want there to be any grounds for reversal. You don't want this bounced to a higher court where the crap you people are pulling on me comes down around your ears and takes your reputations with it."

Then I got up and went over to stand by the window, looking out at the dreary, rainy city, while he told me off. Maybe he'd figured out that when I was facing a judge, I'd be asked who and where my counsel was. And when learning I'd been refused a phone call to my out-of-town attorney, that would either get action or lay groundwork for an appeal. The little D.A. was smart enough to figure all that out.

But right now he was one pissed-off little character. I could sure get the wrong guys teed off at me.

I was still thinking about that an hour later, still convinced a local mouthpiece would be looking out for somebody else's interests, when Chief Belden showed up again, depositing himself on the other side of the bars like he was unloading a wagon load of bricks. A lot of them.

Something had happened to his face. There were streaks in it, like red lines painted on whitewash, and his mouth barely seemed to be there at all, pinched and puckered but with the lips pulled in, like a wound that wouldn't heal.

He had a little pile of fresh clothes in his hands with the shoes of mine they'd taken off me sitting on top. They gave you slippers here so you didn't hang yourself with your shoelaces, like that would work.

"Take these," he said. "Put them on."

I got up and went over to him. I was in my shorts, having shed the pissed-in pants, and was glad for a fresh change. Belden passed the things through to me. They looked a little big, but they were clean anyway. He'd even brought socks.

When I was done, he unlocked the cell and held the door open. "Come on with me, Hammer."

"Got another party going?" I asked him. "Sykes out of the hospital, maybe? Another wet glove job?"

"You speak one more word to me," he said, some tremble in his voice, "and you're gonna get the crap slapped out of you. Come on. Shake it!"

I shrugged and went out the door. At the other end of the corridor, a cop stood by holding the gate open. He was the one who'd worn a gun earlier—now he didn't. And he didn't look happy about it.

This time I didn't get cuffed to anybody, either. Belden just walked me to the booking area and, damn, if there *wasn't* a party going!

Everybody was invited, too—the D.A., the boys from his office, a brace of reporters, everybody clustered in the open area in front of the high booking desk. And this time I wasn't the guest of honor.

That distinction went to one-hundred-thirty pounds of female flesh in a dress, so green it made her hair seem almost white, and so form-fittingly stylish she may have gone to Paris for it. She was being mighty careless with her legs, too, just by having them attached to her body like that.

I had never seen her before, but I'd known this kind of woman—money, breeding, yet all female. And judging by the glowering expressions on the surrounding representatives of officialdom, she had really thrown a wrench in the works.

The D.A. scowled at me, waved Belden over with a crooked forefinger, then stood me in front of the blonde like her prize at the fair.

His face was set as rigid as a bronze statue as he said, "I needn't tell you how imperative it is, Miss Charles, that you make a proper identification. Study him very closely. Very closely."

I didn't get the pitch, but I let her study me, all right. Hell, I'll let any blonde study me *damn* close so long as she looks like Miss Charles. I'd even study her back, and if she'd say something nice about me, I'd say something nice about her, like how well she carried off going without a bra, and maybe ask her in a cheeky way why didn't her panty outlines show like they did on every other girl?

But then I've always had a way with women.

Meanwhile, the thinking part of my mind was wondering why this identification was being made under these conditions. Why hadn't I been hauled to a show-up with a bunch of other cellblock candidates? And why in hell was the *press* here? Since when did an I.D. in a murder case get made like the circus had come to town?

And then even before she had uttered a word, I knew; I knew that she had arranged this. And if she'd arranged it, inviting the reporters along, that meant she was somebody. But why had she done it?

Right now she was frowning gently, her tongue a wet little dart that snaked out between her full dark-red-rouged lips for a moment as she tried to take apart the puzzle that was my face. I knew what her voice would sound like. It had to sound that way. Rich. Not too deep. Rich and sensual and—just to make it more tempting—cultured.

"Well," she said, in a voice and manner that bore out my expectations, "he looks... somewhat different, I admit. His face seems—swollen, sort of. Has he been injured?"

74

Then she looked at my eyes. Hers were gray. They didn't smolder. They didn't laugh or dance or do anything a blonde's eyes should do. They just looked, and that was enough, because she said, "But there's no doubt about it. This is the man I saw."

The D.A.'s fist made a meaty smack against his palm. His scowl became a smile that wouldn't convince any jury.

"Now, Miss Charles, please listen," he said. "You must be absolutely *certain* about this. In circumstances like these, we can't afford a mistake."

She nodded, as if to say, *I understand.*

"Look at him again," the D.A. said, pressing a little. "Take in every detail. See if you can recall the face of the man you saw on the night in question, and compare it mentally with his. Superimpose them in your mind. If there is the *slightest* doubt, then it's your duty to say as much. Look at him *closely.*"

She shifted her weight to both legs now and stared at him insolently. "I *said* he's the same one."

Behind me Belden cursed under his breath. The D.A. threw the chief a helpless look and made a vague gesture with both hands, like a wide end who just missed catching an easy pass.

Reporters were scribbling furiously in their pads and flash bulbs were popping like it was opening night.

One of the assistant D.A.s muttered, "What a hell of a note *this* is."

"Okay, Hammer," Belden said, motioning me with curled fingers. "Come on this way."

I got up, wondering what it was all about. If she had just identified me, why was a fresh witness bad news? Why the hell were the chief and the D.A. reacting like their dog died?

What the hell—I trailed after Belden. No cuffs. No cop trailing.

We didn't go up the corridor. We went to Belden's office and I waited while he fiddled around in his safe and brought out a manila envelope. He got behind his desk and then spilled my watch, wallet and some pocket junk onto his blotter. I looked at him curiously. He looked back with something that might have been boredom or possibly contempt.

Then he shoved a receipt blank across to me.

"Take it and sign for your belongings."

I was getting sprung!

You bet I signed the receipt.

When I reached for my wallet, he said, "Count your money."

"Chief, I'm going to give you what you didn't give me."

"Yeah?"

"The benefit of the doubt."

And I stuck my wallet away.

Then I reset my watch and strapped it on. Finally I lit myself a Lucky and pulled the smoke down deep into my lungs and let it stay there until it came up by itself.

It was a little too much to take all at once. Just a little too much. What all can happen to a guy in a few spins of the Earth? I had another pull on the butt and looked at Belden, who had finally lowered himself into his swivel chair. His face was a pasty gray with a slightly mottled touch here and there.

"What's this angle?" I asked him. "It's not like you boys to be so nice to a sex killer."

He laid his hands flat on the desk top. "Hammer," he said slowly, "I don't know what the hell comes off here myself. You tell me."

"Tell you what?"

"How you managed it! Stranger in town. I'd like to know why Melba Charles, whose old man owns half of Killington, was eating in a hash house at the same time you said you were. You got yourself a very special witness to alibi you out of the hot seat."

My mouth smiled while my forehead frowned. "That's all it takes? Just her word? Nobody else seems to remember me being there. I won't ask if anybody at the diner remembers seeing *her*."

"I know *we* won't be," Belden muttered.

"She sure must be some special character witness, if you take her word for it like that."

Red blossomed over the pasty gray, retaining splotches of purple. "She's special, all right. If it was anyone else, I'd roast the pants off her until I was damn sure she was telling the truth."

"I'm not sure she's wearing pants," I said, hauling out a grin. I didn't have many left the way my poor battered face felt. "So… you do have doubts about it?"

Belden's head made a slow negative motion. "Not even one. She's as reliable and upstanding as they come. Oh, she saw *somebody*, all right. I'm just not convinced it was you."

"For the record, my mother says they broke the mold making me."

He wasn't amused.

I asked, "Does your witness say we spoke or anything?"

Because I sure as hell didn't remember her, though I wasn't about to say so.

Belden didn't answer that, just pawed at the air and made a face like a kid about to cry.

"Get the hell out of here, Hammer! You're free and clear, but if I were in your shoes, I wouldn't leave town till further notice, or we might come looking for you… and you could get dragged back punched full of holes. You know all about that, like you seem to know about a lot of other things, don't you?"

I understood. Go, but stay. Keep handy, while the boys dig up somebody the blonde might have seen who wasn't me at all. Be available so they could give me back my room with its trick electric lock that was reserved for very special customers. I took a real long haul on the butt and flipped it into the desk ashtray.

"I'm not going anywhere, Chief," I said. "Anyway, I got things to do."

"What's that supposed to mean?"

I leaned both hands on his desk. "It means, you got played for a sucker and I got made a patsy. Maybe that's fine with you, but I don't like it. Me, I make a habit of evening scores, and I'll be enjoying the friendly ways of Killington until I settle this one."

The red in his face even overtook the purple now. He shook a thick finger at me and blurted, "You stay the hell out of police business, Hammer!"

"You're forgetting one thing, Belden."

"Yeah?"

I found one more grin—a really nasty one. "You're the one who *made* me police business."

He was thinking about that, the red not fading, as I went out.

It was still raining, so I waited for a minute on the police station stoop beneath an overhang, hoping for a cab. None came by, so I shrugged and stepped down to the sidewalk. My footsteps splashed a little. The rain was cooling and at least it didn't smell like fish. Nobody bothered to tail me. Why should they? Hell, this town wasn't big enough to hide in.

I got as far as the corner when I saw her. She was in a yellow two-door Ford Super De Luxe convertible, the top up, sitting on the passenger side with the window rolled down just far enough to let the smoke drift out. Nobody was in there with her.

Was she waiting for me?

I walked around to the driver's side, found the door unlocked, climbed in behind the wheel and shut myself in.

"Hello, Miss Charles."

She said nothing. Didn't even look at me. With her cigarette regally in hand, smoke escaping lush dark-red lips, she was the picture of sophistication.

I said, "I'll start working on ways to thank you."

She didn't respond so I started the engine.

I asked, "Where to?"

Now she looked at me. Just looked, the lovely face registering nothing at all. "To the courthouse."

"Okay. I owe you chauffeur service, at least. But I don't know my way around this town."

She looked at the rain-streamed windshield and nodded. "It's straight ahead."

I made a face at her. "I'm not much on courthouses. They remind me of D.A.s and cops and things. Pick a better spot."

Nodding back in the direction I came, she said, "I can pick the one you just left… unless you drive us to the courthouse."

Those gray eyes were set off by matching eyeshadow. A fairly heavy, lightly plucked brown eyebrow hiked over her right eye.

I had a strange feeling that I might know what she was up to. But that seemed crazy. I did owe her some attention, considering. So I shoved the car in gear, started up the wipers, and pulled away from the curb.

My pretty blonde liked getting her own way. But what did she want with the likes of me? She didn't have much of a memory, if she'd already forgotten I was just some bum off a freight car. *Memory?* Hell, I wouldn't call it that at all. Imagination, maybe, but not memory.

She never saw me anywhere before, especially not in some hash house. If she *had* been there, I never would have been tossing a line at that streaky-blonde waitress. Maybe her story set the cops on their tails, but she wasn't getting far with me.

"And why the courthouse?" I asked her politely.

The cigarette made a vague gesture, her eyes on the rain-flecked windshield again.

"We're going to be married," she said.

"Oh."

We drove half a block, the wipers providing percussive rhythm.

"What," I said, "and you figure this is your chance to try something new?"

Nothing from her.

I added, "Like find out what a sex killer is like in the sack maybe?"

Her slap caught me in the mouth and damn near smashed the rest of my lips to a pulp. I jerked my head back in time to miss the next one, a little fist this time, and I caught the crazy look of fear and hate that pulled her cheeks tight before my hand cupped her chin and shoved her back. It rocked her against her door and I finished the job with the brakes, bracing myself while she pitched toward the windshield, catching herself rudely on the dash.

I pulled over.

She was too stunned to talk for a good minute, and if I hadn't seen the tears in her eyes, I would have shaken her like the spoiled child I guessed she was.

"Try smacking me just once more, Sis," I said, "and you're going to get paddled but good."

She glanced at me in alarm. Maybe she really didn't have panties on under that green dress.

"Not even a blonde pulls that stunt more than once with me," I said, working to keep the anger down, "even when they lie me out of a jam. I admit I owe you, but I'm nobody's punching bag. Get that in your head and keep it there... Now, do you want to go back where you came from, or do you still want the courthouse?"

She wouldn't look at me. She put one hand to her chin and kept it there, as if checking it were still intact. "The courthouse. Please."

Please.

"Well, that's better," I said. Then I shrugged. "It's your wedding, but you're a sucker to do it, wealthy kid like you. If you're really hankering for the experience, I could pay you off free, no trouble."

"You son of a bitch," she said, mouth trembling, eyes wetter than the windshield, little fists in her lap. "You damn dirty son of a bitch."

"Say that again, baby, and I'll kiss you. Girls who talk dirty drive me wild."

Her eyes got wide. They sure were gray. The dress stretched tighter across the high rise of her breasts and her head shook briefly.

Roughhouse she could stand, but by all means don't kiss her. What a hell of a game this was getting to be.

Lucky for her I didn't believe in long engagements.

CHAPTER FIVE

In a way I was wrong about that long engagement.

This one was going to last a whole three days. The bald little man in the bow tie said so, shutting down any notion of Melba Charles and me just stepping up to a city hall counter and getting hitched. He took down our life history in brief, accepted the three bucks I passed through the window, handed us a medical form to have filled out, and said to come back on Friday, if we were both physically fit and still wanted a civil wedding.

All that without taking his eyes from the counter, then—still filling out the paperwork—he said, softly but pointedly, "Your father isn't going to like this, Miss Charles."

The look Melba gave the top of his head wasn't exactly friendly. "I stated my age as twenty-nine. You needn't advise me about anything."

The pinched face with the little round wireframe glasses came up to confront her stern expression. "That may be the case, Miss Charles, but I feel it's only prudent that I—"

"Can it, Mac," I said.

His eyes seemed to retreat into his head, as he wondered whether to be afraid or offended, then seemed to settle for both as he returned to the form he was completing. You could bet, the minute we went out, he'd be on the phone to the powerful man who made everybody in this town jump.

I guess by now the rest of the story had got around. A killer had been shaken loose on the Senator's daughter's say-so. I was alibied out and the law had to let me go, but it wouldn't make a damn bit of difference to the public. I was their boy, wrapped up and delivered in a blood-red ribbon by the local rags.

But the rags weren't all. This was the kind of town, neither big nor small really—what, maybe fifty thousand fine citizens?—that had a grapevine consisting of party-line gossips, water-cooler know-it-alls and street-corner rumormongers. Twenty minutes since I got sprung, and the town already knew all about it. Another twenty and my impending nuptials would be everywhere. A great place, Killington. Really swell.

In the corridor, I took the blonde by the arm, friendly but firm. A snake might have bitten her the way she jerked away.

"I don't like to be pawed," she said coldly, though the gray eyes blazed.

"I'll keep that in mind. Let's go."

"...where?"

"A doctor, kid. You tell me which one and where. We need blood samples, remember?"

Her mouth tightened just enough to give it a look of wry condescension. But nothing could ever make a mouth like hers anything but beautiful. No matter how she twisted them, those were the most kissable lips you ever saw. Full. Ripe. Damp and hungry-looking. A mouth that wanted to taste you, and that you wanted to taste back.

She could give me her society girl sass but I already knew a warm woman was under there, waiting. What I didn't know was whether she was waiting for me. What exactly she had in mind for yours truly, besides my name on a marriage certificate, remained to be seen.

She knew where to go. She had every single detail mapped out. The doctor was waiting, went through the formalities and told us he'd send the report in at once. He seemed to have something to say but was afraid to let it out. The shaded distaste in his eyes was the same as the little four-eyed guy in the courthouse, though he was not inclined to put it into words.

I was starting to get just a little bit sick of this.

But what choice did I have? If she changed her story, withdrew her identification, I would be slammed back in a cell, with a ticket to Sing Sing and a date with

Old Sparky. I would go along, for now anyway, till I found out what the hell this was about…

At twenty minutes to twelve, we left the doctor's office. The sky was rumbling but the rain had slackened some, enough for us to trot across to where the car was parked. We were halfway across the street when thunder cracked and the puddle to my left parted in the middle, as if an invisible board had smacked it.

Only that hadn't been thunder.

I pitched forward, rolled into Melba's legs, taking her down, and was at her side to brace her when she hit the pavement. She started to claw at her dress, in some spasm of modesty, but I shoved her under the front bumper before she could get the hemline down and she lay there swearing into the rain while she called me every lousy thing she could think of.

I waited a minute, then took a look around the right front tire. This street with its facing row of office buildings was deserted, the gray wet world out there home only to very light traffic, mournful headlights poking through a midday made evening by weeping clouds. I stood up and, for just a second, made a nice target just to be sure.

All it did was rain.

Behind me came the sound of tearing cloth. Melba, trying to dislodge her dress from where it got caught on the bumper, was cursing. At me.

I said, "Will you shut the hell up?"

"Don't you tell me—"

"Get in the car. Stay low!"

"…What?"

"Do it!"

I gave her a shove that ripped her dress loose from the bumper guard, then crawled around to the passenger door and opened it. She slipped inside, crept over and got behind the wheel and I pulled the door shut after me.

Wiping my wet palms off on a nearly as wet shirtfront, I said, "Gimme a cigarette."

"They're in the glove compartment."

I reached in for the deck, shook one loose and stuck it in my mouth. When I held out the pack to her, she turned her head away and said something I didn't catch. Maybe it was just as well, because it couldn't have been nice.

First, I lit the butt. When I had all the smoke in me I wanted, I said, "You know, maybe now I don't have to marry you after all."

Her eyes asked the question.

I shrugged, smiled some. "Could be we're even. Could be I just settled the score."

Her eyes got a little wider. My lord, they were a pretty gray.

"You got me out of a murder rap," I said. "So I'm obligated… or was. In case you missed it, that little tumble on your tummy I gave you probably saved your life."

"What are you—"

"Somebody took a shot at us."

I thought with that I might have gotten more expression out of those big gorgeous eyes. I didn't.

They did the same thing as when they first saw me; they just looked.

"You're crazy," she said.

"Am I?"

My hand found the door handle and opened it. I stepped out and walked to the puddle. I pointed and she opened the driver's door to lean out and see.

The groove on the concrete under the water was like a white chalk mark about eight inches long, a skinny finger pointing right to the curbstone and the little blob of mashed lead I was looking for. I went over, picked up the irregular slug, walked back to the car and got in.

I opened my hand. "Pretty, isn't it? Offhand, I'd say it was caliber .38 and damn good shooting, considering it was a handgun at some distance."

This time I got something from the eyes—lovely gray eyes that were a little anxious and a little afraid at the same time. "We're... we're *not* even."

"Aren't we?"

She didn't have to say it. I knew exactly what was coming and she could have saved herself the trouble. "You didn't save my life, not if somebody was shooting at *you*."

Then it was my turn to say the obvious. "Were they, Blondie?"

The raindrops in her hair sparkled. It matched the wetness of her mouth and the glints of anger in her eyes. She said, "I'm thinking that maybe it wasn't you I saw in that diner the other night. I'm thinking I ought to tell the District Attorney so."

I gave her a showy shrug. "I'm thinking you didn't see me the other night either, kid. So I'll call you on it. Take me back and we'll tell the D.A. about it."

I leaned back against the seat cushion, took a last drag on the butt, and dropped it out the window.

"You're clever, aren't you?" she asked softly.

I nodded. "Clever is a good word for it, sugar. Shrewd is even better. No beautiful babe is going to haul a bum out of a murder rap unless she *wants* him for something… and I'm betting you want me for something."

The last grin I had in me met a frozen stare.

"Any time you want to go back to jail," she said, "say the word."

Who was calling whose bluff?

"Un-uh," I said. "No, I'll stick around a while. I got me an awful curiosity. I'm waiting to hear the rest of the proposition. It must be a honey. Now take me someplace. *You* play pretty chauffeur—I don't know the town well enough to do the job justice."

Amusement almost registered on the lush lips. "Where to?"

"First to a fleabag where I left my baggage the other night."

Very businesslike, she kicked the engine over, snatched the shift lever into low and jerked out into the street. A lot of leg was showing thanks to her ripped dress, and she didn't seem to care. I certainly didn't mind.

I told her where I thought the place was and she turned off into a series of side streets, met an intersection and swung left. I spotted the bar where the trouble all started, picked out the sign over the doorway of the hotel, and nudged her to stop.

The bleary-eyed clerk looked at me, trying to place my face. His clip-on bow tie was hanging again, but on the other side, real loose, as if that scab was finally ready to fall off. The cigarette he had going actually had tobacco in it this time.

I passed over the key to the room and said, "I never made it back. I got a bag up there."

He gave me a look like I was nuts. "She ain't there *now*, mister."

"I mean a *real* bag."

He checked the key number again, muttered, "Oh," under his breath, then went in back and returned with my overnight case.

"You're lucky, pal," the clerk said. "One more day and this woulda got sold. You owe me a buck for storage."

He got a buck and I got the bag. I went back out to the street and tossed the case in the back seat and closed myself in. There was still something else to do—the important something.

I told Blondie to ease down the street and, when I came to the spot I was looking for, hopped out again and went down the cellar steps and poked around the cracks in the cement, trying not to let anxiety take over.

It'll be here, I told myself. *No reason for it not to be.*

And it was, all right—thirty thousand bucks in brand-new thousand dollar bills. Relief flooded through me like sunny warmth on this dismal damp day.

This one thing going right—the reason I'd come to this lousy burg in the first place—was what really counted.

I stuffed the packet in my shirt.

Melba looked at me curiously when I got back in the car. Maybe it was the relieved satisfaction on my face that got her thinking.

Her eyes became suspicious slits, the gray peeking out. "What was *that* about?"

"Not your business."

"You *are* my business, Mr. Hammer."

I grinned at her. "Once we're hitched, Miss Charles, we may want to switch to first names."

She was shaking her head slowly, the arcs of white hair swinging just a little. "I don't know what you were up to over there, but I don't like it."

"And I don't care. I wasn't trying to please you." I gestured toward the rain-spattered windshield. "Okay, it's your show now, so let's get on with it."

The little shingled cottage was about five miles outside of town with a graveled drive leading in from a blacktop road. The impression I got, mostly from the overgrown grounds, was that nobody had used this place in some time. And also that it was nothing special.

She pulled up in front of the door and cut the motor. We sat for a minute, then I said, "Love nest?"

Her glance had irritation in it.

She got out. I pulled my suitcase over the back of the seat and did the same. We walked up and she plucked a key from her handbag and unlocked the door. We went in.

I was all wet in thinking nobody had been there lately. From the outside it didn't look like it, but inside it bore a woman's touch. The place was done in mountain style with knotty pine walls and a fieldstone fireplace, and there wasn't a speck of dust anyplace as far as I could see. The novels in the built-in bookcase were recent and the ashtrays were clean. The furnishings dated back ten or twenty years, but they'd cost real money—this was the kind of casual that rich people enjoyed.

When I'd dropped the overnight case to the floor, I pulled out another Lucky, lit it up, and sat down. It was all so nice and homey, with her going around lighting the lamps. That is, until you remembered that this was strictly tinsel, a too-real stage setting that had little lead bullets mixed up with it somehow.

She turned the lamp on by the window and stood there fiddling with the shade. The light came up from the top, making a halo of her hair and doing things in shadow that I hadn't noticed before. There was a lot of her I hadn't noticed before, either. Like how almost mouth-to-mouth tall she was to me, and how her legs filled out the nylons and rose into firm, rounded thighs. She must have sensed the tear in her dress, and closed it without thinking, the movement of her arm a graceful gesture that accentuated the breadth of her shoulders and lengthened the hollow that dipped below the neckline of her dress.

It was too bad, I thought, that she had to be such a damned phony. Any other time and she would have been a beautiful woman with all the promise that implied. But she was a phony, all right. I was getting the build-up with sex on display but not on the menu, and was supposed to be sucker enough to stick around for what might come my way. Whatever kind of curve she was getting ready to toss was going to be a doozy.

Hell, it *had* to be. She was putting a lot of lovely hide on parade all for me, but she didn't seem to know that when you over-bait the hook, a fish can yank you right into the drink.

I squashed my Lucky out in the ashtray. "Now we talk."

She still held her dress together, too casually. "All I want from you is your name for a while. You behave yourself, there will be a financial settlement, when the time comes. Say, ten thousand dollars?"

That was some dowry.

"Okay," I said. "But what's it about? Don't I have a right to know the score?"

"There isn't anything you need to know." She glanced at me to see how settled I was, then sat down at the end of the sofa. "It should be enough that you're out of the hands of the law."

I shook my head. "Oh, but that's not enough, Blondie. I would have gotten out anyway."

A "V" formed between her eyebrows for a second, then disappeared. "You sound confident for a vagrant who just crawled out of a jail cell."

"I may not be the bum you take me for. I may be somebody who would have arranged a Manhattan lawyer to prove I never bumped that dame. And I never raped a woman in my life."

The pretty mouth made an ugly sneer. "Is this where you say, 'I never had to'?"

I frowned at her. "I never *wanted* to. File that away, sister. That piece of information could come in handy to you."

She shifted on the sofa, looked down her well-carved nose at me. "I'm to believe you didn't kill that woman? That you're innocent? But isn't that what they *all* say?"

"Yeah, but—"

"And now you're telling me you're the exception? No, I did better than just read the papers. I had someone find out every detail of the circumstances and I don't think there's any doubt about what happened. You killed that woman."

"You don't seem too worried about keeping company with a killer then."

"Why should I be? Aren't I your only excuse for being free?"

She had a point.

"And as long as *I'm* alive," she said, "*you* stay alive."

"If I really killed that woman. But suppose I didn't."

Her eyes narrowed. "Then there's no reason for you to do me harm," she said. "Either way, you're no threat to me."

I gave her the nastiest grin in my repertoire. "Are you sure? How about a fate worse than death?"

At first, she was going to come at me. I saw it in her face and the clawed set of her fingers. Then she said, "You said it yourself. You're no rapist."

"Is a husband who consummates his marriage a rapist? I don't think that way, but I might make an exception for an heiress with a fortune I could get my grubby fingers on."

She went damn near as white as her hair. She was afraid. Not of the killer she claimed she thought I was. But of the man sitting on the couch with her who was fed up with being manipulated.

"Don't worry about it, kid," I told her, grunting a laugh, pawing the air. "Right now I'm too tired to do anything except play word games with you. I can wait. Hell, it's only three days."

A horrified kind of loathing pulled her cheeks tight until she looked like some kind of Oriental cat.

"If you ever touch me," she said so softly I could barely hear, "I'll kill you."

The nasty grin again. "Honey, please—a cultured type like you knows it's polite to wait till you're asked."

"*Bastard!*"

Now she did come at me with those clawed fingers and I knew I'd gone too far. I had her wrists and she was all big eyes and flared nostrils and clenched teeth, and my options were to kiss her or slap her, which was when I began to feel like a real jerk, and did neither, shoving her back into the cushions at her end of the couch. She curled up into herself, frightened, obviously realizing this whole thing had got out of hand. I just smoothed my shirt and looked around for my composure.

So I thought about this damn crazy situation for a while. I tried to figure the angles but all I got was curves. She sat there with her legs tucked up under her to get as far away from me as she could. I plucked another cigarette from the pack and sat back, now looking at her.

"Okay, Blondie, give it to me straight," I said. "No fooling around. Too damned much has happened and I don't feel like being messed with. What's behind all this?"

With a frustrated frown, she said, "Can't you just be satisfied with your freedom?"

"No." I held a match up to the end of the Lucky. "Being married isn't exactly freedom."

"It's better than jail."

"I don't know." I caught her eyes and they never wavered. "Maybe it will be—later."

Her voice held contempt. "You'll never know," she said.

"Maybe," I said, shrugging, "but that isn't answering my question. Let's start at the beginning. Let's start with

Senator Charles, who owns the fish cannery stinking up this lousy town."

"He's my father."

"Yeah. I picked up on that. So you have money and social standing. Plus, you're a hot-looking number who can attract any kind of man you want, yet you snag one out of the clink with a screwball story and hold it over his head to make him marry you."

She seemed offended. "I don't see why you should complain about it."

"Baby," I said, "I'm complaining all right, and loud. I don't like being tapped for a kill, I don't like being mauled by a pack of smalltown cops, and I especially don't like being suckered by some babe who's got a deal cooking I fit into some way that she won't say. No matter how I look at it, it's me who's left holding the bag. Now *that's* what I know. What's the rest of it?"

She gestured with open hands. "Nothing. I told you everything in the first place."

"Damnit! You told me nothing!"

She shook her head. "All you have to do is marry me. Nothing else. I don't expect, nor will I ask of you, anything else. After we're married, you can do whatever you please. And then there's that ten thousand dollars."

I took the butt away from my mouth and stared at her. "Let me take a wild stab at this. You've been with some bad boys in your time, and over the years, Papa's been disapproving—chased them off, bought them off... that kind of thing?"

She was smiling now. "You *said* you were clever, Mr. Hammer."

"And this is your revenge. Run off and marry an outright murderer. What a beautiful way to tell the old man to go screw himself."

Her shoulders lifted and came back down. "Clever and shrewd, you said."

This time I shook my head slowly. "Fine. Swell. But explain away the bullet in the rain, honey. It could have been *you* it was meant for."

"But it wasn't."

"Convince me."

Her open-hand gesture was graceful, very Country Club, as was the expression she gave me, chin lifted.

"The Warburton girl," she said, "has two very violent brothers. One of them already shot a man for making advances at her. Went to prison for it, though he's out now—the spurned suitor was only wounded, you see. The brothers have been threatening that if the state doesn't kill you, they will."

CHAPTER SIX

My bride-to-be fixed us a little supper. Whether cooking skills could be added to good looks, among her wifely attributes, remained to be seen—for now she just opened a can of Dinty Moore stew and heated it up in the little kitchenette off the living room.

While she did that, I had a look around the place. At the rear was a bedroom with more lodge-type trappings—framed hunting and fishing prints, rustic pine furnishings, log double bed with a comforter with a cloth grizzly bear sewn on. Not that grizzly bears are all that comforting.

Across a small hall was the john with shower plus a storeroom with water heater, washing machine, and electric furnace. At the end of the hall was a rear door onto a little patio with a grill, and a small garage was back there, too, a gravel drive leading around to it. Beyond, land rose steeply, trees and brush holding on for dear life, the forest so all-encompassing you had to crane your head back to see any sky.

I joined her in the kitchen area, where the beauty in the green Paris original was playing what's-wrong-with-this-picture as she put down plates of stew and two bottles: beer for me, 7 Up for her.

We both sat at the little round maple table. A kind of wary truce had settled in.

"We'll have to rough it till I can get some fresh supplies tomorrow," she said apologetically, passing me a little basket of saltines in lieu of bread.

For a guy who'd eaten K-rations in Pacific foxholes, this kind of roughing it was not a challenge.

"I don't live here," she said.

"I didn't suppose you did."

"I have an apartment in town, but sometimes I like a weekend with the out-of-doors all around. That's not anything I advertise, though. So for us, I think staying out here makes a lot of sense—reporters won't likely find us."

She hadn't seemed to mind reporters when she brought them along to embarrass the D.A. into quickly releasing me.

"Or that dead woman's brothers, either," she added.

That much was a benefit.

I said, "You sound like you want us to spend the whole three-day waiting period out here."

A forkful of stew froze, midair. "I think that might be wise, yes."

"Why, so we can get to know each other better? Honey, I didn't come to Killington for my health."

"What *did* you come for?" She really just seemed to want to know.

That rated a shrug. "Personal business. Nothing to do with you. But I need to be mobile. How about you be a nice kid and fix it so I can rent a car?"

She frowned, returning the forkful of stew to the plate. "I hope you don't have any plans to go looking into this thing."

I figured she meant the Warburton girl's murder, but I didn't ask. I just said, "No. I said it was personal business and it is."

Like being framed for murder and rape wasn't personal.

Her expression was so intense, her eyes focused on me so tight, she might have been about to scream or maybe burst out crying.

So I gave her just a little bit more. "I need to look up the wife of a guy who was in my outfit overseas. It's not a big deal, but it's a promise I need to keep."

"Can't it wait?"

"It already *has* waited—I didn't figure on getting arrested for a sex kill, not to mention having a socialite propose marriage."

She blushed. Actually blushed.

"Is *that* what you think I am?" she asked, very quietly. "Some rich-girl refugee from the society page? Me, the daughter of a *fish cannery* magnate?"

I shrugged again. "Daughter of a senator."

She smiled a little and poked at her food, seeming too embarrassed to meet my eyes right now. "Daddy was a state senator for a single term, a long time ago, back when *his* daddy… my late grandfather… was still running the family business. Ever since then, he's been 'Senator' Charles. But Senator Charles is just a small-town big wheel who runs a cannery, going back generations in the family, and *that's* whose daughter I am."

"How about the fish glue works? Your daddy owns that, too, doesn't he?"

She pushed her plate of stew away, little of it eaten. "He does. But my brother Lawrence is in charge."

"Any other potential in-laws I need to know about?"

She shook her head. "My mother died when I was fairly young. There's just Lawrence, Daddy and me… well, Lawrence is married with two children. Very respectable, my brother."

Any time somebody is described as "very respectable," I start to wonder.

"You and your brother get along?"

She rose, plucking up her plate and taking it to the sink, her back to me as she said, "Of course. Why wouldn't we?"

Something about that made me wonder, too.

I asked, "You have a role in the family business?"

"No."

"What *do* you do?"

She was getting a bottle out of a cupboard—

Smirnoff vodka. "I don't do anything. Serve on a few charitable committees. Go down to New York to see plays and shop. Travel. Nothing, really."

But she was no rich-girl socialite, right?

With the bottle in one hand and a water glass in the other, she returned to casually pour herself a good four fingers into the glass. Then she added some 7 Up as she settled back down.

"Sometimes I go club-hopping," she continued. Then the gray eyes flashed. "If anybody asks, that's how we met. At the Copa, maybe. Or the Latin Quarter."

I shook my head. "Nobody will buy that. Guys who hitch rides on freights don't hang out at nightclubs, unless they're a dishwasher or push a broom. I have a better one."

She was all ears. "Oh?"

"We met a couple years ago at a USO dance." I swallowed some beer. "Felt the ol' mutual attraction and wound up spending the whole rest of my leave together—translation, we shacked up. After that we wrote letters back and forth."

She was nodding now. "Yes! And you came to town hoping to re-connect, but got swept up in that murder thing first."

"And you saw my picture in the papers and came forward to get me out of a jam. But, no… scratch that." I'd been cookin' but then the cake fell. "It doesn't jibe with you seeing me in a hash house. *That* story makes me out a stranger. And it's on the record."

Half the glass of vodka and 7 Up was gone. "You don't understand yet, do you, Mr. Hammer?"

"Mike."

"Mike. I'm the Senator's daughter. Once I came forward, you were off the spot. People may question my motives, they may think I'm lying and gossip about it all over town, while the police and the District Attorney and his staff whine about miscarriage of justice…" She sipped and smiled. "…but nobody'll do anything about it."

"If you say so."

"I do. Anyway, leave out any indication we… shacked up. Or even that we kept in touch. We met at the USO, the Stage Door Canteen… I'll say I was helping out. We spent some time when you had a pass or a leave or whatever it is."

I nodded slowly. "And after I got mustered out, I came to town to look you up."

She smiled big, seeming pleased with herself, and toasted me with her now almost empty glass.

Seemed like a good time to try again. "So, how about helping out a guy you met at the USO? With some wheels?"

"You can use my old Packard," she said, off-handedly. "It's in the garage out back. You need any money?"

Here was my opportunity to become a kept man, but I said, "No. I'm fixed. I'll try to take care of that personal matter tomorrow, okay?"

She nodded. "All right."

After all that chatter, we wound up spending the rest of the evening like any married couple—not talking. Melba drank her vodka and 7 Up while I ran through the beer in her fridge, as we sat on the couch listening to the radio—Baby Snooks, Ginny Simms, Jimmy Durante. Also, *It Pays to Be Ignorant*, which hit a little close to home. Back in the city about now, the drinking was being done in gayer circumstances. But that was for people still looking for a mate, or escaping theirs.

Around ten she fixed the couch up with a pillow and a light blanket, then headed off to her log bed and its grizzly bear spread. We said good night, politely, even pleasantly, first names and all. The truce was holding.

Yet somehow I knew that if I headed back to that bedroom, she'd have something waiting to shoot me with.

The day dawned sunny.

The world out here past the city didn't seem to have low-hanging clouds, no gray rags overhead sopping with rain, ready for wringing. We were so far away from civilization, the fish stench was only the faintest memory. And the sounds of late summer in the forest were at it like a symphony—chirping birds, buzzing insects, croaking frogs, and somewhere a brook was babbling. In town the chirps came from chippies, the buzzing came in entryways, and plenty of croaking and babbling was going on, too, none of it at all symphonic.

I got some coffee going. Cream of Wheat was in the cupboard and I boiled some water and got a couple servings of that going, too. She came out yawning, stretching, the white-blonde hair nicely askew, the curves wrapped up in a pink terry-cloth robe that couldn't have looked better unless you were tearing it off of her.

She seemed amused seeing me at it in the kitchen. "Maybe you'll make a good husband, after all."

I gave her the lopsided grin. "Don't push your luck. I hope you socialites like it black, 'cause there's no cream."

"Black is fine."

"There's sugar, of course."

"No need."

She sat at the little maple table and I served her up, then joined her.

"I may be away much of the day," I said.

"Your friend's wife need that much attention, does she?"

"I want to buy some things. Drive around and get to know your charming town a little better. Why don't you do like you threatened and pick up some groceries. I'll let you make supper."

"This isn't bad," she said, sampling a spoonful of the hot cereal.

"It'll be better with milk. Be sure to pick some up."

She grinned. The first time, a nice grin with fine white teeth in it. "We're like an old married couple."

"Yeah. We don't have sex, either."

She tried to frown at that, but then she could only

laugh. "You like steak? I'll get you some steak. How about a nice big juicy T-bone?"

"Naw. Make it filet mignon. What's the use of having a rich wife if you can't go first class?"

She took the first shower, and I stayed out in the kitchen listening to the sound of it, imagining what she must look like in there, wishing I were the soap. When she came out in the pink terry-cloth wrap again, a towel turbaned over wet hair, I collected my shaving kit and a change of clothes from my battered excuse for a suitcase and had my own shower. A cold one.

When I emerged, Melba had keys for me—to the car in the garage and the cottage.

"Stay out of trouble, Mike," she said.

Something like actual concern was in there. Of course, she had some special kind of need for me that I didn't understand yet. I just knew it wasn't the kind of need a man wants a woman like her to have for him.

Still, hearing her say, "Mike," wasn't bad at all.

Like the cottage, the garage was a shingled affair that didn't look like much. But the "old Packard" turned out to be a silver-gray 1940 180 Club Sedan, as beautiful as the blonde who considered this a "second" car. I got in and started it up and that baby purred. The seats were pleated and plush—there was plush carpeting, too—and when I pulled out and guided the buggy around to the gravel road, I felt like I was sitting on a comfy couch and somehow driving at the same time.

Suddenly marrying a fish cannery owner's daughter had yet another appeal.

The only bad thing about it was, I looked like somebody who would have stolen a car like this. I would have to do something about that.

As soon as I hit town, it started looking like rain again. The highway turned into the main drag, Broadway, at the dingy end of which I found a row of pawnshops. In the first one I tried, a friendly old guy with Coke-bottle glasses, a mangy sweater vest and a witch's mole sold me a .45 Colt automatic with a well-worn shoulder sling and a .38 Smith & Wesson revolver with a new ankle holster. He giggled, thinking about the fun a youngster like me was clearly about to have.

That had swallowed a hundred bucks whole, but a bargain considering, and a sporting goods store in a more presentable section of Broadway was happy to sell me boxes of ammunition. I asked for an oversized sack and, back in the car, put the holstered guns in the sack, leaving the ammo behind.

I kept the sack with me when I dropped by a haberdashery in the most respectable stretch of the street. I had to try several suits on in the dressing room to find one with a fit that would accommodate the shoulder-holstered .45. All of the pants were fine for the ankle one. I bought an extra suit in the same size and cut, and also picked up a couple of neckties, a felt hat and a trench-style raincoat.

Back on the street, even the sodden gray clouds and the fragrance of fish couldn't keep me from feeling— for the first time in this damn town—like myself again.

Maybe that was why next I tooled the Packard to the police station, feeling almost cocky. Not so cocky that I didn't leave the weapons in the car, though. I didn't have the paper along to prove it, but I was licensed to carry in this state, so if push came to shove, I could do the pushing. But why borrow trouble?

Chief Herman Belden had no outer office nor any female manning a desk outside his door. You just knocked on the wood and pebbled glass slab and took your chances you'd catch him. I did that, and his bellow bid me enter.

Belden glanced up at me from behind his big oak desk and frowned. Not a scowl, just a frown. He didn't know me at first, not shaved and with the swelling gone down. But then came an expression of surprised recognition.

"Where did you get the money for those kinda threads, Hammer?"

I shut the door and helped myself to that comfy chair across from him, happy not to be cuffed to anybody's wrist this time.

Crossed my legs, folded my arms. "Haven't you heard? The Senator's daughter took one look at me and had to have me."

The chief tossed some reports aside and leaned back in the swivel chair, rocking a little. He was in his rolled-up shirtsleeves and that purple tie again, which went so well with his mottled complexion. His smile was nothing to write home about, just a thick-lipped thing, also purplish.

"Yeah," he said, scratching his head with its less than bumper crop of hair, "I heard congratulations are in order."

I grinned. "I figured that little jerk at City Hall wasn't going to sit on something that juicy."

Rocking gently, he said, "Sounds like you got it made, Hammer. All that money and respectability wrapped up in a dish like that. All you got to do is live till the three-day wait is over."

"Funny you should say that," I said, and dug my right hand into my suitcoat pocket. I found what I was looking for and flipped it onto his desk, where it tumbled to a clumsy stop on his blotter.

He frowned down at the mashed-up slug. "What's this?"

"Somebody took a shot at me yesterday. That's what's left of the bullet."

He picked it up and rolled it around between his thumb and middle finger, giving it the kind of attention a jeweler does a diamond. "Not much left for the ballistics boys."

"No. I figure it's a .38, but who knows? It scraped itself on the cement on its ride and hit the curb and got all bent out of shape. Sort of like you cops when you had to spring me."

Belden smiled at that. "Little late reporting it, aren't you, kid?"

"I'm not reporting it at all. It's just something I'm sharing with a guy who's the only cop in town I trust a little."

No thick-lipped grin now. No frown, either. He was just studying me, the way you do a suspect that you're starting to believe, much as you don't want to.

"You really didn't kill that girl, did you, Hammer?"

"I didn't. Hell, I didn't even rape her. I'm just that good a citizen."

He kept studying me, little glittering slices of his eyes staring out of slits. "Just what kind of citizen *are* you?"

"What do you think? Solid."

"I thought I saw something about you that was off, that first night. For a guy riding the rails. But I sloughed it off. Only there was something about you... something almost... cop."

I shrugged a single shoulder. "Run my name past the NYC boys and see what you find."

"Why don't you save me the trouble."

"Mind if I smoke? Now that you don't want me to burn anymore."

He answered by getting a cigar from somewhere and lighting it up while I did the same with a Lucky. Our smoke drifted together.

"I was a cop, briefly, when I got out of service," I said. "Did well in the academy, but I got in trouble on the street."

"Take one too many free apples?"

"Pounded too many bad ones. They stuck me on a desk and I quit. About a month ago, I opened my own shop."

His eyebrows went up; the eyes weren't slitted now. "You're licensed?"

"And bonded. Full private investigator's ticket. Also licensed to carry in New York State."

He chewed on that, and the cigar. Then: "Want me to spread the word?"

"I do not."

He chuckled as he savored a mouthful of corona smoke. It streamed out as he said, "I figured as much. Not considering the way you came to town. You were trying to slip in under the radar, only it didn't work out. Why did you come to Killington, anyway?"

"I had a favor to do for an army buddy. That's all I can tell you, other than it has nothing to do with the sex murder."

"You really didn't know the Warburton girl?"

"I did not."

Telling him I'd seen her sleeper-window striptease was nothing I cared to explain. Cops hate coincidences, which they shouldn't, because life is full of them.

"Well," he said, sitting forward, looking genuinely confused, "if you don't want me spreading the word that you're a private eye in town on a job… and that if a gun is found on you, it's state-approved… why are you talking to me at all?"

My turn to let out some smoke. "I need someone I can trust on the inside."

His purple-lipped smile had a sneer in it. "You said before that you figured you could trust me. That's a big leap of faith to take in a godless town like this, son."

"I know it is. Only… when I was in custody, I watched you. You're tough and even a little mean, but on a department where guys like Sykes are the standard, you're a rare bird indeed. And without somebody I can ask a question to, now and then, I'm taking a tour of Killington in the goddamn dark."

Belden nudged the spent slug with a finger. "Maybe you're just distracted, wondering who might want you dead, besides most of the cops in this town."

I sat forward. "I think I already know. The dead girl has two brothers who in the past didn't like it when guys got frisky with their sister. Somebody who raped and killed her would really get the royal treatment."

He was nodding. "That's a fair assessment."

"So what's the story on this pair?"

He thought about whether to answer that or not, then gave a what-the-hell shrug and dove right in.

"Alf is the oldest at around forty," he said. "Rex is the baby at thirty-eight or -nine. Alf missed out on the war, doing time—shot a guy."

"Guy who messed with his sister."

"Yes. A guy who messed with his sister. Rex didn't serve, either. He flunked the physical, only the reason wasn't physical—he's what the medics call a psychopath. Three of his girl friends died under mysterious circumstances, only nobody around this building finds that mysterious."

"Makes for a peculiar champion of womanhood, if you ask me."

He folded his hands on his belly. "Well, Alf and Rex won't ask you anything. They're likely to send you another of these." He nudged the bullet again. "And another and another, till you can ask those girl friends of Rex's yourself what happened to 'em... assuming you go to the same place as those girls, which maybe's not a safe assumption."

"Maybe not," I admitted. "So what do the bereaved brothers do for a living?"

He gestured vaguely at the window behind him. "They were at the cannery for a long time, but they got canned, so to speak, for running Sunday crap games— both the cannery and fish-glue factory are closed on Sundays, and the Warburton boys took advantage of that. Alf was a foreman and had keys to both."

"When was this?"

"Well, they got their walking papers around '39. They bought a bar on the waterfront with some of the proceeds of their crap games. Crow's Nest, it's called."

I frowned. "Alf shoots a guy and then gets a liquor license? That sounds strange even in this twisted town."

"It's Rex who has the license. Ran it alone while his

ever lovin' brother was in stir. Now they run the dive together. They can fix you up with a girl with a side of gonorrhea, or some rotgut that won't strain your wallet, assuming you don't mind risking goin' blind."

"Ever consider shutting them down?"

He shook his head, smirking sourly. "They're on the list."

"What list?"

"What list do you think? Anybody who goes into that hell hole knows what they're risking. It's not my job to protect people from their own stupidity. Anyway… they're on the list."

I didn't press. I got up, gave him a nod of thanks, and headed out.

His voice caught me at the door. "Hammer! Where can I reach you?"

I thought about that for a moment, then said, "At Melba Charles' cottage. I don't know the number, but she's got a phone there."

"I didn't know that kid had a cottage."

"I bet a bloodhound like you can sniff it out."

He chuckled at that, then said, "That bar those boys run, the Crow's Nest? You can trust the beer, at least. You could stop by for a quick wet one, and explain to the brothers how you didn't kill their sister. I'm sure they'll listen to reason."

Shutting the door behind me didn't stop the sound of his laughter. In fact it rattled the pebbled glass.

CHAPTER SEVEN

A CLOSED sign was propped in the greasy window under some switched-off electric beer signs surrounding a slightly bigger one that apparently stayed on night and day—CROWS NEST in cursive neon glowing a muted red except the "NEST" had lost its gas and turned a sick milky white.

Between dirty smears I could make out a bar over to the right with a guy behind it who had a row of bottles of name-brand liquor lined up like a firing squad. He was pouring some brownish liquid into them from a tin gas can, using a funnel. It was taking all his concentration.

The place appeared otherwise empty. There were no stools at the bar, just a foot rail and a couple of spittoons. I could make out sawdust on the floor, a bunch of banged-up round tables with chairs piled on them, and some half-baked decorative touches like draped fishing net, a rotted-looking life preserver propped on pegs, and a terrible wall mural of a reclining redhead in nothing but a ragged red smile and what was apparently supposed to be a sailor hat. The cartoon crows Heckle and Jeckle had been painted by the same Michelangelo to one side of the naked redhead, eyeing her and dripping saliva from their beaks.

This was only one of at least half a dozen bars in an area of one- and two-story buildings, some brick, some frame, all ramshackle, dating back to the last century. The ragtag collection of union halls, secondhand stores, pawnshops, warehouses, diners, and saloons made the rougher parts of Killington I'd already visited seem like the Upper East Side. The Charles & Company Cannery and its fish-glue offspring were a few blocks from here, the smell of their industriousness thick enough to slice and stuff in a can and call it sardines.

The door, which had its own smaller CLOSED sign, was unlocked. So I went in—never could take a hint.

The guy behind the bar frowned at me. He was in a dirty blue work shirt and probably stood six foot two, his two-hundred and twenty pounds or so of gristle and sinew distributed around a wide-shouldered frame; his hair was dirty blond and unruly. His mouth had already been hanging open, but it managed to hang open further as the tiny close-set peepers crowding his nose opened with the wide-eyed innocence of a newborn suffering its first gas pain.

"Can't you read?"

"Can't you?"

He thought about that and spilled a little of whatever he was transferring into a liquor bottle from the gas can.

"You a cop?" he asked, taking in my suit. "We paid already this month."

"Maybe I'm from the health department."

"This ain't gas! It's just that kind of can."

I crossed the sawdust to the bar and put a foot on the rail. "No, I figure it's bourbon or maybe Scotch or just good old-fashioned rye."

"You do?"

"Yeah. I mean, it's what you're filling those bottles with. It's all whiskey in the end, right? Anyway, I'm not health department."

"You ain't a cop, so what *do* you want?"

"I'm looking for the Warburton brothers. I understand this is their place."

"Well, I'm one of them. I'm Rex. But I told you we ain't open, so unless you got business, you need to come back at four."

"I wanted to talk to you about your late sister."

The little eyes got big. "Reporter, huh! We talked to a couple of you bastards, and Alf and me did not like what you wrote."

"So then you *can* read."

He thought about that, too. Then he frowned. "What the hell do you want, anyway? Funeral was two days ago. Leave her rest."

I leaned in a little. "Not a reporter. But since you saw the papers, you should have seen my picture. Take a good look—I cleaned up some, and where I got worked over, the swelling has gone down. I'm the guy the cops collared for what happened to your sister, but I've been cleared. I think you guys may have the wrong idea, and I want to clear this thing up."

He frowned again, deeper. The little eyes almost disappeared. It was like a nose was looking at me. "You're that Hammer guy."

"Yes. And—"

He hit me with the gas can.

Swung it hard and fast, landing with a metallic *whang!* and caught me on the side of the head, sending my hat flying, rotgut splashing, a damn good sucker punch for such an idiot, and I went down like a three-legged cardtable.

Rex was big and he was stupid but he was fast, and he came around that bar on the run, work boots clomping under frayed denim, growling like the dumb animal he was, with a baseball bat ready to hit a home run with my head.

And as he came, bat high, he yelled, "*Aaaaaaaaalllf!*"

I was down between tables, in the sawdust, where I'd landed on my side, my head spinning, but when he got near enough to swing, I kicked straight out, the heel of my shoe catching his left knee. That took the world out from under him and tossed him onto the floor and the bat got hurled God knew where, and now he was the one eating sawdust, right next to me. He turned over, spitting shavings, and I gave him an elbow in the throat that started him gurgling. He was still down and I was halfway up when his brother—the Alf he'd called out for—came barreling out of the backroom. He had dark curly hair, eyes dark in an angry clenched face that looked dirty from need of a shave; stuffed in a lumberjack shirt and denim trousers, he was not as tall as Rex but every bit as burly, though he had a gut on him, so he wasn't as fast.

He paused just long enough to size up the situation, seeing his younger brother on the floor, clearly put there by this stranger in a suit, and that gave me time to sink a fist into his belly past my wrist and double him over, like he was bowing to me. Then I gripped my hands together and slammed them down into the back of his neck and he went down to dine on sawdust, too.

But arms from behind came looping around me and hugged, hugged hard, and suddenly that blond dope's face was pressed next to mine, cheek to cheek like Fred and Ginger.

"Get up, Alf! It's *him*! It's that son of a bitch who killed little *Jeannie*!"

Alf got to his feet slowly, kicked a table out of the way, and gave me the kind of snorting look a bull gives a matador. He started his charge and was almost on me when I threw my weight backward with Rex right behind me and took him down with me, landing on him hard, his grip loosening. I squirmed free and rolled away. While the younger one was down there on his back with the air knocked out of him, hands and legs flailing like an upended turtle, the older one was lumbering toward me with fists like the heads of ten-pound sledges. I was still on the floor, so I kicked out with both feet, catching his ankles, rolling out of the way as he went down on his face like a bridge helped by dynamite charges.

On my feet again, I went over and started kicking Alf in the stomach. Behind me, I didn't see Rex get to his feet, but when he kidney punched me I felt his presence all right, and the pain went through me like a hot poker. I swung around and threw an elbow in Rex's throat and sent a hard underhanded right into his balls. That took him backward into a table and he collapsed with it, chairs tumbling. He was down there crying now, hands gripping his groin in that protective way that is always too late. His older brother was puking, which is why sawdust comes in handy on the floor of a hell hole like this.

I frisked them both, while they were indisposed, and found a switchblade on Rexie and on Alfie a .38 revolver in his back waistband—almost certainly he'd taken that shot at me yesterday. I collected both weapons, feeling lucky that when his brother called out for him, Alf hadn't realized who was out here causing trouble. If he knew, he'd have come with the rod out and ready, and maybe that sawdust would be soaking up red stuff leaking out of me about now.

I brushed myself off. Where the rotgut hit the fabric, the sawdust clung. The suit would need cleaning. Shit. I retrieved my hat, brushed it off, too. Alf had stopped puking, so I went over and kicked him in the side a few times. Nothing gets a guy's attention like a few broken ribs.

Rex was leaning on an elbow, thinking about getting up, or he was till I kicked him in the head and put him back to sleep. That kind of thing can kill a guy, but Rex was breathing, and anyway there wasn't enough in that skull to suffer much damage in the first place.

Alf was on his back, breathing hard. At the side of him where he hadn't puked, I leaned in, resting a knee on his belly, which tightened up and gave me some support.

"I didn't rape your sister," I said, "and I didn't kill her either. Got that?"

He spat blood at me. Got in on the suitcoat!

Damnit!

Time for playtime to be over.

I got the .45 out from under my arm and Alf's eyes widened at the cannon-like size of the thing and his bloody mouth opened wider than his eyes, and I shoved the snout of the .45 between his teeth, letting the gun sight carve the roof of his mouth a little on its way to where it stopped just short of making him gag.

Alf was shaking his head a little—not much, the .45 barrel he was eating didn't allow for much motion.

I said, "If I had killed your sister… if I had raped your sister… wouldn't I blow your head off now?"

His eyes got even wider, wondering the same.

"I should do it," I said, "just to pay you back for taking that potshot at me yesterday."

His eyebrows tightened and fear and sorrow got together and pleaded for his life.

"But I'm not going to blow your head off," I said. "Or your numbskull brother's. Because I didn't kill your sister or rape her or any damn thing. It was just another frame-up in this crooked town."

I got up. They stayed down. At the door, I said, "If I had done it, you'd be dead now. You get that don't you?"

Rex was still out, but Alf nodded.

"But come after me, and I *will* kill you. Don't make me sorry I was nice. Understood?"

Alf, still on his back, nodded.

Rex was coming around. "...what?"

"Tell him," I said, holstered the rod and went out.

Wouldn't you know it?

You buy a new suit and the first thing that happens is you get it messed up brawling. So I tooled the Packard back onto Broadway and found a one-hour dry cleaner, where I changed into the other suit I bought and went off to find a diner for lunch to kill time while I waited out the cleaning and pressing job.

A corned beef sandwich and fries, and a vat of black coffee, made me feel human again. It occurred to me there was somebody I owed a phone call, since this Killington stay had extended itself in unexpected ways. The plan had been to sneak into town, deliver my war buddy's dough to his missus, then—assuming no unexpected problems arose—take the bus back. No need to put myself through another dance recital with the railroad dicks.

But I had a good friend back in the big town who I'd left dangling, and I owed him an explanation, or anyway enough of one to pass. I couldn't go into great detail, because Pat Chambers was a patrolman with the NYPD and I couldn't risk sharing everything.

He and I had gone into the service together, though wound up in different outfits, and when we got out, we enrolled in the academy and started on the department at the same time. But he was better than I was at sticking to the rules, and was making a go of it. I'd struck out on my own, where I could make my own rules.

The bus station was just down the street and, after getting a couple of bucks turned into change at the diner, I headed there. In the waiting area, I settled into one of a row of telephone booths and started feeding the operator quarters and dimes.

Pat lived with his folks in Brooklyn. I got his mother. "Is Patrick home, Mrs. Chambers?"

"Yes, Mike, but he's sleeping. He's working nights, don't you know."

I didn't know, but I said, "Wake him up."

"Oh, he'll be mad as a wet hen!" Then she gave me a sigh that turned into a laugh. "But he'd be madder if

I didn't. He's been tryin' to get a hold of you for *days*, and you've got him half out of his ever-lovin' mind!"

"Well, shake him awake, and tell him it's long distance. No time out for a stop at the john—he can do that on his own dime."

"Oh, Michael, you're a rascal!"

"All the girls say so, Mrs. Chambers."

Pat was on the phone within a minute, and he already sounded wide-awake. "What the hell's wrong with you, Mike? You leave town and don't even tell me! And what's this crap about a murder charge? And rape? Jesus!"

"And how are you, buddy? Your concern touches my heart. I got cleared of both charges, thanks."

"You're still in Rhode Island?"

"Yeah."

"You're lucky it isn't Sing Sing. What kind of job are you on, anyway?"

"A job my client wouldn't care to have shared with somebody in a blue uniform. Look, I just wanted to check in with you and tell you I was okay."

"Well, that's fine, that's swell. I must've called your office, what, a dozen times? Why don't you get yourself a secretary?"

"I'll think about it."

"You have any kind of idea what you've stirred up? What kind of trouble you're in?"

"I ran into some up here, but I'm on top of things."

"Really? Well, I got hauled in to talk to some dicks

on the robbery detail about you. What's this about you being the last person to talk to Bob Lewis in the jail ward at Bellevue… maybe an hour before they draped a sheet over him?"

"Bob and I were friends overseas. You know that."

"I'll tell you what else I know. He was in custody after getting shot by a security guard when he robbed Evello Vending Company in Queens. The cops caught up with him, bleeding, a couple blocks away. Do I have to tell you who Carl Evello is? Or that his vending-machine outfit is a syndicate front?"

"I don't know anything about any of that."

"The people at Evello Vending say Bob got away with a few hundred dollars. Do you believe that? You do know that your old pal was part of that mob before the war—and that he'd have been in the perfect position to know when some real money was in the safe. Not nickels and dimes from coin machines, but the green stuff casinos and prostitution and narcotics generate."

"Pat, I'm gonna run out of nickels and dimes myself. This was just a courtesy call, buddy."

"Don't 'buddy' me. What's going on, Mike? What part do you have in this? Please tell me you haven't gone over to the other side."

The cop on the door knew me. He was my age, and Pat's, another beaming young Irishman from our graduating class at the academy. When I told him Bob was a friend of mine from army days, he let me right in. He didn't realize that when Bob was allowed a phone call, the call hadn't been to a mouthpiece, but an old war buddy.

I knew at once he was dying. He had the sunken cheeks, the gray skin, the watery eyes, but most of all he had the look.

The look.

The look we'd seen when one of ours took enough rounds to make the outcome unquestionable. The look that saw past everything into what awaited. The look that wondered if Heaven and Hell were a myth and only a big empty awaited.

But then the look turned into something else, something with some sparkle in it when he saw me. I didn't sit. I just leaned in and rested a hand on his pillow next to where his head was barely making a dent. Christ, he must have lost a lot of blood. Several bottles were hanging like shrunken heads feeding something into his veins.

"There's easier ways to get rich, kid," I said.

He nodded. "I know. I screwed up. I got greedy. Not… not a bad kinda greedy, really. I got greedy for my kid."

"What kid? You get married when I wasn't looking?"

I hadn't seen him since maybe a month after we got back.

"I met a girl," he said. "She lives up Rhode Island way. I moved up there. Got a job, decent job. But when she told me she was expecting, I wanted something better. For her. And for him or her or whatever God gives us. And I knew about some easy money."

"Yeah. I heard. You hit your old boss's favorite money laundry. For a few measly hundred."

He grabbed my sleeve. The hand looked skeletal but the grip was full bore. "No. I got over thirty grand, Mike."

It was a whisper that screamed.

"It's under the seat of my car in a parking lot about two blocks from where the cops picked me up."

"There's a lot of parking lots in New York, boy. You remember a name?"

He did and gave it to me.

"Get it," he said. "Get that dough and give it to my wife. Her name is Mitzi Loomis. I changed my name up there. Bob Loomis. But for God's sakes, Mike, don't lead them to her! Sneak in, sneak out. If they find out whatever you're up to, you're dead. And so is she. And so is... my kid. Promise me, Mike! Promise me!"

I promised him.

"Look, Mike... this isn't a favor. You're a private operator now. Yeah, yeah, I kept track of you. Proud of you, man. You didn't screw up. So this is a job I'm asking you to take on. Help yourself to a grand and whatever expenses you rack up."

"Don't be silly."

"Damnit, Mike! I'm not going out of this world owing anybody anything... Well, the cops won't get what I owe them, and I can live with that. We got a deal, Mike? We got a deal?"

"We got a deal."

"One last thing... Mitzi, she don't know anything about this. She knows Lewis is my real name, yeah, and that I wasn't always an honest working stiff. But she thinks I'm down here seeing friends. Knows nothing about the score. And if I don't make it, Mike... and let's face it, I ain't gonna make it... she won't even know. I'm not a story that'll make the papers, out of state. Tell her I'm gone, Mike—you tell her."

"Now you are asking a lot."

"But you'll do it, won't you?"

"What do you think? But this wife of yours—she's not going to want to take this kind of loot."

"I know. You tell her... you convince her... it came from friends and relatives, passing the hat."

"Sounds like a big hat."

"Make her believe it, Mike. And she'll be upset, not being at the funeral and all..."

"Quit talking like that. You aren't dead yet."

"Now who's silly? You just tell her that I wanted to be buried in a family plot at Woodlawn. That she can visit me some time, my next birthday maybe."

"Does your brother Bill know about Mitzi?" The rest of his family was gone.

"Yes." His eyelids were sliding down like blinds being pulled. *"When... when things settle down, he can... get in touch with her."*

"Bob, I know you think you have this all worked out. But she's bound eventually to find out the circumstances of your..."

But he was asleep.

He had summoned all the energy left in him for this meeting, and there wasn't any more. I had everything I was going to get from him.

I nodded to the cop outside the door and went out. My pal was dying, but that part of it wasn't my business. I knew what I had to do.

Pat said, "The robbery detail guys think your buddy Bob pulled down a major score, and the Evello bunch is covering up, since money laundries don't advertise. Do you know anything about that, Mike?"

I ignored his question but asked one of my own. "How did you know I was in Killington?"

"The robbery dicks told me. I'm just a lowly patrolman, but detectives like that can check the wire and see what's shaking state-wide."

"So what if they can?"

"So you maybe've heard the rumor that the syndicate boys have certain… resources on the department. That means if the NYPD knows about your situation up north, so does Evello and his crowd—who probably also know you were in conference with Bob Lewis right before he went."

"And these robbery detail boys were specifically asking about me?"

"Oh yeah. I'm your friend, remember? Nice to know while you're out getting yourself killed, you're ruining my career."

"Who says I'm out getting myself killed?"

"Oh, I'm saving the best for last, chum. The robbery guys say the word is the Two Tonys are looking for you. You've heard of the Two Tonys, right? Tony Pigozzi and Tony Scarnetti? Evello's favorite torpedoes. Seems they're on the road. Looking for somebody. I wonder who."

The operator interrupted, wanting another twenty-five cents. I didn't give it to her.

Pat said, "*Mike!* You get your tail back here! I got friends on the department who can give you protection—"

But the call had ended.

CHAPTER EIGHT

First the two Warburton brothers, now the Two Tonys. The animals were coming at me two by two. Now I knew how old Noah felt, particularly with another gray sky floating overhead, dark clouds moving at a slow boil.

This flashy Packard didn't exactly make me hard to spot, and swapping Melba for her yellow Ford Super De Luxe convertible wouldn't be an improvement. My rearview mirror didn't report anybody on my tail, but I couldn't risk calling on my buddy Bob's fresh widow, not till I knew this new threat was dealt with.

The last thing I wanted to do was lead Evello's boys to her.

So I headed back out to the cottage to re-group, and found another conspicuous car pulled in on the little gravel skirt out front. Snugged next to Melba's Ford was a sleek black Alfa Romeo, one of the new post-war jobs that I'd never seen in the flesh before. But more guys drooled over pics of that baby in the auto mags than they did over Rita Hayworth in *Esquire*. If you have ten grand, you can have one, too—the ride, not Hayworth.

I pulled around back and left the lowly Packard at the mouth of the garage. While I didn't figure the Two Tonys were driving around in a machine like that, I was taking no chances—it *was* Italian, after all. I got out of the raincoat and draped it over my left arm and unbuttoned my suitcoat, to give me free and easy access to the .45 in its sling. Then I came cautiously around the cottage to try to find the right window that would tell me who belonged to that black beauty.

The window onto the kitchenette did the trick.

Listening intently, Melba, in a pale yellow blouse and white slacks, was seated at the little round table across from a well-groomed guy of maybe thirty-five in the kind of sharply cut charcoal pin-striped suit that goes well with an Italian sportscar. The same was true of his slicked-back black hair and his broad-shouldered but slender physique.

They were having coffee, and his hand was on top of hers. Old boy friend maybe, here to talk her out of the mistake she was about to make with some out-of-town bum...

Couldn't see his face—his back was mostly to me, he leaning in to her, she leaning in to him. Then Melba noticed me in the window behind him and, after a tiny look of surprise, motioned me to come around to the front door.

She met me there and her guest came along. His features were familiar—they echoed Melba's own, with a masculine cast that still possessed a near long-eyelashed prettiness, and a tan you only got with plenty of vacation time. Like when you're the boss. And that smile of his was broad and white, so perfect he either had a hell of a dentist or an in with God.

"Mike," she said, "this is—"

"Lawrence Charles, Mike," he said, his voice smooth and deep. "Melba's big brother, *only* brother actually."

We shook hands, his grip firm but not showing off.

"Pleased to meet you, Larry," I said, taking the same liberty he'd taken with me.

The smile remained but tightened a little. "I prefer Lawrence. Perhaps you prefer Michael?"

"No. If you're not my mother, it's Mike."

He gave that the laugh it didn't deserve, then my bride-to-be's brother led us to the couch, playing host. Melba sat, tucking her legs under herself, and I dropped in next to her, not too close, while Lawrence pulled up a chair and settled in, facing us. His loafers were as Italian as his sportscar, and he was drenched in a cologne I recognized: Canoe. But for all his best efforts, some fish smell was making its way into the boat.

"So," he said, "I understand you kids met at the Stage Door Canteen. The USO! So romantic, like something out of the movies."

I was looking for sarcasm or any hint of an inflection that might indicate his disapproval. It wasn't there. A bum rolls into town riding a box car and now is about to marry this guy's sister—another mouth at the wealthy Charles family trough. And he seemed fine with it.

"Yes," Melba said to her brother, her smile overdoing it, "we exchanged a few letters, while Mike was overseas, but imagine my surprise when he turned up in town."

Imagine my surprise when I was framed for rape and murder. And imagine my surprise when the town's favorite little rich girl gave me an alibi and a marriage proposal.

"Well, it's an unusual story, all right," Lawrence said, with a quick roll of the eyes. He got out a silver cigarette case and selected a smoke, then offered me one and I took it. He produced a matching silver lighter and fired me up. The cig was strong, even harsh, but I liked it.

He read my reaction and smiled as he gave himself a light. "French smoke. Gauloises. Best in the world, I say."

And only the best for Lawrence Charles.

"D'you serve in Europe," I asked, "and pick up a taste for these there?"

His face lost all expression for a moment, then his mouth half smiled, the Gauloises bobbing in the other corner. "No, I didn't serve. Flat feet, I'm afraid."

Or maybe connections on the draft board.

"One of the great frustrations of my life," he went on. "But I must say I admire you for your service,

Mike. I hear you won the Bronze Star."

"I came out of it breathing and that was the point of the exercise."

He stowed the smile away. "And you were on the police, too, I understand, in New York City?"

Was Belden his source, I wondered, or had it just gotten around the well-greased Killington grapevine?

"Briefly," I said. "I was declared over-enthusiastic and wound up on a desk, and that's not my style. I opened up an office of my own and now I'm still mostly sitting at a desk. But business will pick up."

He was nodding. "I'm sure it will. We're moving into some real prosperity in this country, although frankly my family's business did well even in the Depression. People have to eat, and canned foods like ours fit a lot of pocketbooks."

Enough to buy Italian cars and shoes, anyway.

He leaned in and patted his sister on the knee. She looked away, as if the gesture embarrassed her. "Mel tells me you haven't talked about where you'll settle down. Were you thinking of staying with your little detective agency, and living in the city? Perhaps we might tempt you with a job here in the fishing industry."

I inhaled the strong smoke, held it, let it back out. "I've caught a few in my time."

The smile was back. "Are we talking bad guys or fish, Mike?"

"I was talking fish, but that does work both ways. Your sister and I will talk about this, obviously… but

I don't think I'm the executive type, if that's what you're offering."

That seemed to offend him, just a little, but the smile didn't falter. "I wasn't exactly offering anything, Mike. I was just…"

"Fishing?"

He chuckled, raised a shoulder in a half shrug. "I only wanted to drop by and let you kids know I'm behind you all the way. Marriage is such a wonderful institution."

Was it Groucho who said, *But who wants to live in an institution?*

The cigarette was in his fingertips and he made smoke trails as he gestured. "I've been married for fifteen years, Mike, very happily. Eva's a wonderful girl and we have two boys, one six, one ten, and they really make all the hard work worthwhile."

Yet somehow the Alfa Romeo didn't strike me as a family car.

"Eva's great," Melba blurted, the smile still looking forced. "And the boys! Wild Indians but so sweet."

"And we don't have a governess, either," Lawrence said, raising an eyebrow. "Eva does it all herself. She's a treasure."

"A *national* treasure!" Melba said.

She seemed a little nervous, sitting there with her arms folded and her legs tucked under her, as if she were trying to make herself as small a target as possible. Maybe having to trot out the story we'd concocted about how we met had thrown her a little.

"You have a nice set-up," I told him, "assuming you don't mind being tied to the family business. Did you ever want to go into anything else? My old man had a bar and when I turned my back on that, he didn't speak to me for a year."

"I had ambitions," Lawrence admitted, the smile more relaxed now. "Wanted to be an actor, if you can believe that."

He had the looks and mellow, radio announcer voice for it.

"But the Old Man encouraged me to help him expand the business," he said, "and after college, I came up with the idea of using our cast-off scraps and skins for a glue factory—and he was enthusiastic right off the bat. He backed me all the way and it's been hugely successful from the start."

"I never heard of fish glue, frankly."

He shrugged. "It's no different from using the remains of horses and cows. Instead of ears, tails, scraps of hide, tendons, and bones, we process bones, heads, scales, and skins of fish from our cannery."

Melba shifted uncomfortably.

But her brother was on a roll: "We wash and soak the resulting stock, and cook it in open vats, into what we call glue liquor. It thickens into jelly."

"Honestly, Lawrence," she said, "Mike doesn't care to hear you talk shop."

Lawrence frowned at his sister, but I spoke up.

"No, this is interesting," I said. "Anyway, I like to see a man with a genuine interest in his work."

Lawrence gave me yet another smile, and a nod, and said, "Anyway, these are early days for you and me, Mike. We have a lot of getting to know each other to do. I just wanted to assure you that however... *unusual* these circumstances might be, my sister has my full support. And that means *you* have it, too."

"Well, thanks, Lawrence. That's real nice to hear."

Lawrence let out a sigh, patted his thighs, then stood. "And speaking of work, I need to get back to it. Melba, thanks for the coffee. Mike, would you walk me out to my car?"

I said sure, and he took me by the arm as we strolled to his sportscar. When we were there, he said softly, "Mike, the Old Man wants to talk to you. Nothing to be leery of—he just wants a word. Surely that's understandable in a situation like this."

"There is no rule book," I said, "for a situation like this, Lawrence. But I'll be happy to talk to him."

"Good. He's at the house right now. It's on the Bluff." He handed me a folded slip of paper. "There's the address and directions. Go alone."

Then he smiled at his sister, who was in the doorway, got into his fancy ride and glided away. And, yes, even on gravel that thing could glide—it was that smooth.

But then so was its driver.

* * *

Already I was lying to my intended. I had told her I was going into town to try to connect with my army buddy's widow. Instead—wondering if I was about to be offered a pay-off, or possibly have my life threatened—I was calling on the patriarch of the family fortune, who ruled atop the Bluff.

The Bluff was where the new wealth of the first half of the last century had staked out the best views of Killington Bay for their lavish dwellings. Early on, this part of the country had plenty of dough in lumbering and saw mills, and flourished as an agricultural center; but by now this was really a one-industry town, unless you counted the cannery and the fish-glue factory as two.

So it was no surprise that among sprawling gingerbread mansions, some looking a little long in the tooth by now, the near-palace of the Charles family had a block to itself, right at the top, sitting in a private little park of manicured shrubbery and magnificent maples. Residences on the downslope reflected their corresponding incomes until at the foot were slum housing.

But of course the Charles place was no slum. The stately L-shaped limestone Federal Colonial, three stories with a two-story wing, wore a cedar-shingled roof with two chimneys, red shuttered windows, and a white-pillared porch, its double front door crowned with transom windows.

The brass bell was the kind you pulled and chimes pealed within. I waited for admittance, expecting a butler. I got someone else.

He was as tall as me and half again as wide, but not really fat, his bulk well-packaged in a tailored gray suit with a pale-blue tie, his white shirt as crisp as the white smile in the broad oval face. His nose was wide, the nostrils ready to pull in enough air for two men, his salt-and-pepper eyebrows untamed, his eyes the same pale blue as his tie. His hair managed to be thinning and bushy at the same time, and as white as the shirt and the teeth.

"Mike!" he said, his voice the same baritone as his son's, only with a sandpaper edge. "I'd know you anywhere."

He shoved a hand at me like a gardening tool going into moist earth and I took it. His grip might have popped my fingers like toothpaste tubes if I hadn't been ready for it. Senator Charles may have been born to money, but those hands had worked. Maybe his daddy started him scaling fish or working on a fishing boat with netting and gaffs.

Him "knowing me anywhere" only meant he'd seen photos of his prospective son-in-law in the paper, and the only trick was recognizing me when my face wasn't swollen up from the wet leather glove treatment.

"Senator Charles?" I asked.

"Yes. But we're not going to stand on formalities, and we'll certainly drop the honorific. I'm Ernest."

Was that a noun or an adjective?

"Your son prefers Lawrence to Larry," I said, as he ushered me in with a fatherly arm around my shoulder. He smelled of Old Spice, not Canoe. "I'm going to guess you're not an 'Ernie.'"

The half smile he gave me was wider than most full ones. "No. Never did care for that. Never even heard it used till this last war—Ernie Pyle and all. To that degree, my son and I are both a little old-fashioned."

We were crossing a surprisingly narrow if high-ceilinged entryway, with a formal living room through a wide archway to my right, and a library to my left, a hallway hugging the second-floor staircase straight ahead. Everything was grand, but unpretentiously so. This was one of those George Washington Slept Here houses.

He steered me to the library and deposited me in an overstuffed leather chair. I was asked if I'd like something to drink and said beer.

"Excellent choice," he said, and went to a trawler-size desk and used a phone with several lines. He said to someone, "Would you bring two beers for our guest and myself? Thank you, dear."

The walls were all books, mostly the leather-bound kind nobody reads, but near the desk, whose swivel chair's back was to some front windows, the volumes were a twentieth-century mix of fiction and non-, and catalogues and magazines were stacked. A half dozen four-drawer wooden file cabinets were grouped back there as well.

He saw me looking as he plopped down across from me on another brown leather chair. Four of these were arranged mid-room around a coffee table with a number of popular novels piled casually— *Drums Along the Mohawk*, *Northwest Passage*, *For Whom the Bell Tolls*, and half a dozen others.

"I do most of my work here at home," the Senator said, as if admitting a shameful secret. "That's a liberty I take as owner and chief high muckety-muck. Oh, I go in to the plant twice a week, where people can get at me. A man can't duck all his responsibilities." He came forward conspiratorially. "But I tell you, Mike, I simply cannot *abide* the smell of fish."

I laughed. "Well, that would be a drawback in your line."

He chuckled and leaned back, his hands on the arms of the leather chair; he looked like the benevolent dictator he apparently was. "Some people don't mind it, the fishy fragrance. Some people don't notice it, after they've been around it long enough. But it still registers on this old schnozzola."

A short heavy woman with a pretty face and nicely coiffed medium-length blonde hair trundled in with two bottles of Rheingold and two pilsner-style glasses on a tray. She wore a yellow-and-white house dress, not the black-and-white livery of a maid. She poured the beer with professional aplomb and gave me a nice smile, and nodded at her boss. Calling her pleasantly plump would have been a stretch, but you could see she'd been a knockout once.

He thanked her and she paused a moment, somewhat hopefully, as if expecting a tip or something. Then she went out, vaguely disappointed, as he raised his glass to me. "To my future son-in-law."

I raised my pilsner. "What growing boy couldn't use a rich father-in-law?"

That only made him smile, though I'd said it to needle him a little.

"You must be wondering why I'd take a stranger in with such open arms," he said. His face was one of those ugly ones that was pleasant to look at. "Well, I am happy to have my daughter finally settle down and make a real woman of herself."

"Sir, there are few women any more real," I said, "in my experience."

"Oh, she's a beauty, all right. But the girl has never settled down nor shown any sign of ever doing so. Her mother died when she was young, so there wasn't much guidance. Oh, I don't mean to imply she was... wild or anything. She just didn't... land anywhere."

We both sipped beer.

He said, "You must have looked pretty darn good in uniform to make the impression you did, back there at the Stage Door Canteen."

The story had got around and everybody in the Charles clan seemed eager to buy it.

"Seeing the jam I was in," I said, "must have touched her heart. Somehow she knew I'd come to town to look her up, and felt she had to come forward and help me. She did, of course, and we just... clicked."

"And the rest is history," he said, with a sage nod.

How could he be buying this baloney? She lies me out of stir, and right then falls head over heels and—poof!—we head to the courthouse?

"I know you must be concerned, Mike, that Melba's original story… having seen you that night… might be questioned by the authorities. Now that she's about to marry you—the soldier boy she fell for in such a storybook fashion—one might expect them to be… suspicious."

"One might," I said.

"But as you may have guessed," he went on, shrugging casually, "I have a good share of influence in this town. I can assure you that you'll be left alone, and that my daughter won't be challenged. The alibi will stand."

"Good to hear."

He leaned forward again. "I, uh… spoke briefly with Lawrence on the phone. He said you seem reluctant to have us find a place for you in the family business."

I waved that off. "Your daughter and I haven't got that far yet, sir."

"Not 'sir.' *Ernest.* I did some calling around, Mike, and have learned of your war hero status, and your brief career as a… shall we say, controversial officer with the New York constabulary. And how you've only just recently opened your own office."

I drank some beer, nodded. "That's right. You may have learned that I'm licensed and bonded, too."

"Yes. Good for you, son. But I wonder if you might consider moving your operation here to Killington. I could help you do that."

I shifted in my leather chair. It made a rude sound.

"Sir… Ernest… that's generous. But an area this size can't really support my kind of business."

He gave me a smile Macy's Santa Claus would have killed for. "You might be surprised. You'd have no competition here, and the cities and towns and hamlets of Rhode Island and Connecticut might avail themselves of your services. We're not that far from Boston, either, you know."

The hard sell.

"Ernest, I'll give it serious thought. Will that do for now?"

His nod was enthusiastic. "Of course it will. And wherever you lovebirds alight, I hope you'll consider giving this old man a few fresh grandchildren to bounce on his knee. My daughter will be thirty soon and she needs to stop spending all her time flitting around shopping and going to Broadway shows and dating this one and that one, and… well, she needs a *real* man in her life. And you clearly fit the bill."

He stood and extended his hand again for a second shake. I was being dismissed, but in a nice way.

"I have to get back to work, son." He rested a palm on my shoulder as he walked me out of the library and back into the entry area.

I was outside and almost to the car when I felt another, smaller hand touch my shoulder.

I turned and there was the maid or housekeeper or whatever-the-hell-she-was, all blue-eyed and pretty but too damn hefty for me to care.

"Yes?" I said. "Did I forget something?"

"No, Mr. Hammer." Her voice was high-pitched and breathy in a nicely feminine way. "I just wanted to make sure I hadn't been rude."

"Rude?"

"Not speaking to you. My father-in-law is a good man, and kind, but sometimes where women are concerned, he can be, well… provincial, and a tad thoughtless. He should have made an introduction."

I lifted a pointing finger. "You're… Eva?"

She smiled. That really was a beautiful face. She extended a gentle hand, its nails bright red. I took it, held it a few moments rather than shake it, and its softness was nice.

"Yes, you met my husband, earlier. I'm the little woman."

No comment.

"We live here with the Senator, Lawrence and the two boys and I," she said, bright-eyed. "You know, Lawrence was favorably impressed with you, and he isn't always."

That sounded like I'd done well at an interview.

"I just wanted you to know," she continued, "that I'm really thrilled for you and Mel… really *thrilled*!"

"Well, thanks."

Eva clasped her hands to her generous bosom. "She's a lovely girl, but never had much luck with men… till *now*, I mean. I'm so happy for her. You'll make a really lovely couple."

We did sound… lovely… didn't we?

"Eva… may I call you Eva?"

"Please. And I'll call you Mike."

"Yeah, that'll work. May I ask you something? Why is this family so damn welcoming? I'm nobody special. I was sitting in stir facing rape and murder charges a couple of eye blinks ago."

Her expression took on a disturbing blankness that robbed it of much of its beauty. She looked over her shoulder, perhaps making sure her occasionally thoughtless father-in-law wasn't spying.

Then she moved close and whispered, so hard to make out I had to lower my head to her moving lips.

"There's something you need to know," she said.

"What would that be, Eva?"

"I was with Lawrence that night."

"*What* night?"

Her eyes widened. "Why, the night the Warburton bitch got what she deserved. Lawrence was with me the whole time! How's *that* for an alibi?"

Then she gave me a kiss on the cheek and ran back to the porch and into the house.

CHAPTER NINE

I got to the cottage just as dusk was settling in, the overcast sky a threat as yet unfulfilled. The threat of the Two Tonys also remained, my rearview mirror giving no sign of anyone on my tail through the afternoon. That dropped me into an uncomfortable limbo—how could I contact Bob Lewis's widow without risking exposing her to the wrath of the New York mobsters?

But after one more day here in Killington, I would be expected to head back to the courthouse with my blushing bride and fulfil our bizarre bargain. Otherwise all the goodwill being showered on me by the Charles family—not to mention the benign neglect of the Chief of Police and the D.A.—would come to an abrupt end.

Part of me wanted to trust Belden not to let that happen, but with men like Sykes on the force, I could wind up resisting arrest and arriving D.O.A. before any rare honest cop in this cesspool of a city might clear things up. And when you're dead, being exonerated falls a little short.

She met me at the door with that white-blonde hair brushing her shoulders and her mouth as red as a new wound, and I'll be damned if she wasn't wearing a frilly white apron. Beneath it was a light-blue blouse, a string of pearls against pale skin, and a darker blue skirt dotted white. She was that picture of a happy housewife you saw all the time in the slick mags and never once in real life.

"I've been grilling," she said.

"That's a coincidence," I said, stepping inside as she made room for me. "I've been getting grilled."

She didn't ask what I meant, instead just told me to join her on the little patio in back. Along the way I shed my raincoat, suitcoat, tie, shoulder- and ankle-holstered rods, putting the hardware at the bottom of the stack, as Melba didn't know about them yet.

Outside, she sat me down at a small slatted wooden table and served me up a filet mignon from the grill. There was also corn on the cob and a baked potato, both wrapped in foil. Butter and salt-and-pepper shakers were already waiting, and a small salad with Thousand Island dressing. A sweating bottle of Knickerbocker beer was placed before me like an offering to the gods. Or one god, anyway.

Melba had a smaller filet for herself and corn on the

cob, too, but no potato. Her salad had just a dollop of dressing. A homemaker had to watch her figure or else she might wind up like Eva Charles.

It was perfect—the steak bloody, the salad dressing tart, the potato and corn cooked long and slow. I ate like the king of the castle, or of the shingled cottage anyway.

She watched me, pleased to see me enjoying myself. All that was lacking was her asking me how work had gone, and had I asked the boss for that raise?

Apple pie à la mode was the coup de grâce.

"I got it at a bakery," she said, looking a little embarrassed and even guilty.

"You're forgiven," I said, as I put away a second slice.

My flitting little socialite could cook. Maybe marriage wasn't a fate worse than death. I didn't even mind helping her with the dishes. Hell, I volunteered. But I didn't wear a damn apron.

Neither did she, by the time we were sitting together on the couch, Melba tucking her bare legs under her again. Out the windows, night had fallen, but no raindrops yet. I was smoking a Lucky. She was having one of her own, a Marlboro, one of those brands aimed at women.

She said, "It's starting to feel like fall."

"Yeah. Getting nice and crisp out there. You want a fire in the fireplace?"

"That would be nice."

I built one, got it going.

When I returned, she had maybe moved a little closer to where I'd been sitting. Maybe. That meal was the nicest bribe a man could imagine. Well, the second nicest.

In the orange glow of the flames, she looked impossibly beautiful and vaguely sad. I didn't help that any when I said, "I saw your father today."

Her sharp head-turn toward me said something, but I wasn't sure what. Her actual words were, "Didn't you see that woman? Your army friend's wife?"

"No. There's a hitch to that. I kind of fibbed earlier. Your brother told me your daddy wanted a word with me, and seemed not to want you to know about it."

She was looking into the fire. The flickery reflection turned her into an old-time movie actress. "Oh," was all she said.

"Don't you want to know what he wanted with me?"

"Is it… my business?"

"Who else's business would it be?"

"Well… yours."

"I'm your fiancé, remember. It's *our* business. Anyway, it was just more of the same."

"More of the same what?"

"More of the same soft soap your brother lathered up this morning. How happy the Senator is to have a real man as a son-in-law. How pleased he is that you're settling down with a bum who rides the rails."

"That's not what you are."

"No. I guess, in fairness, he did check up on me. Knows I'm an ex-cop with a private operator's license and an office in Manhattan. That didn't stop him from trying to make a fish cannery executive out of me."

She frowned at the fire. "That isn't part of the deal."

"What is the deal, Melba?"

"You know what it is. Ten thousand dollars, when the time comes."

"When will that be?"

"We'll know. When the death of that girl has either been resolved or forgotten."

"That could take a while."

"Would it be so bad?" she asked. "Being married to me?"

"Being married to you would be lousy."

That shocked her and she turned to look at me, hurt in her expression, the half of her face near the fire shimmering, the rest in darkness. "Am I so… awful?"

I held my hand out as if to touch her face, but let the fingers float there, inches away. "No. You're wonderful. That's the problem. Being married to you… forbidden to touch my own wife… honey, that's hell on earth."

She looked away, hugged herself, as if fighting off a chill, though the warmth of the fire contradicted that.

"Why don't you tell me, doll?"

"…Tell you what?"

"What this is really about. You're caught up in some kind of cover-up for your family. For your father, for your brother. I met your plump little sister-in-law, and she seemed intent on telling me where your brother was the night of the murder."

"Did she."

"Honey, how do I figure in? What the hell kind of role could I be playing?"

Staring at the fire, she said nothing for a long while. Maybe a minute, and that's longer than it sounds. But her eyes were moving. She was thinking. She was considering.

Then she turned to me and did something startling— she touched my hand, which was resting on the couch between us. The time she'd slapped me had been much less of a surprise.

Her eyes pleaded and, like the overcast sky out there, threatened rain. "Mike, could you please trust me? I think… am I imagining things, or do we like each other? Are we friends? Could you do me a favor and just go along? I mean, there's money in it for you, and—"

My hand went to her face and she flinched a little, as if I might strike her, and maybe the thought of me touching her was just as bad. But my fingertips rested gently on her full lips, touching their red stickiness.

"It's not money," I said. "Not now. I don't really know what it is, baby, but money it ain't."

And I kissed her.

Softly, gently, and it lasted a while. She didn't resist but she didn't help out, either.

When our faces parted, she didn't slap me. She was giving me a look of… alarm, I guess.

I said, "That was just my way of telling you how I feel. I won't do it again unless you ask. Or you do it yourself."

Now she gave me another endless minute of a stare. Wheels turning.

Finally, her lovely face again half in flicker, half in shadow, she said, "Mike... you remember that first day, when you... you shoved me. You got rough with me. Twice."

"Yeah. I'm not proud of it, but I remember."

"You have to promise me something. *Really* promise me."

"Okay, sugar."

"No roughhouse. I can't abide that. If you hit me I might... I might kill you."

"Well, we can't have that."

She grabbed my hand and squeezed. "Promise me, Mike. Gentle. Only be gentle. I can't have it any other way. *Promise me.*"

This she said as her hand gripped mine hard, then finally released.

I touched her cheek, the one in darkness. Stroked it gently, ever so gently.

"I promise," I said.

She began to unbutton the blouse.

She took her time, then let it hang open for a while, the twin globes of her high full breasts only partially revealed. Then she gave a shrug and the garment slid to her waist, where she flicked it to the floor. The creamy flesh danced with flames, the smoothness of her a living canvas for a tapestry of dancing orange and blue and red and yellow, the erect centers of those lovely mounds unmoving amid the swaying reflections, yet demanding attention just the same. I gave it to them, but gently, kissing the tips and they seemed almost to kiss back, then the fullness of her breasts filled my hands to overflowing and my body demanded attention, too, a physical change in me not lost on her. With a surprisingly wicked little smile, she started unbuttoning my shirt for me. I let her do that, but then took over, getting out of the rest of my things. She sat there with quiet pride, waiting patiently, watching with hooded eyes, her knees spread beneath the skirt. Naked now, I leaned over and my right hand traveled up a silky thigh.

With the dress hiked to her waist, a bulky belt now, a clump of cloth between so many smooth surfaces, she leaned back, head against the arm rest, and I did some exploring, with my hands, with my mouth, flicks of the tongue, fingertip caresses, always gentle, always tender, because this girl would recoil at anything suggesting roughness, and when the time came, and the tapestry played its devil dance on the flesh of us both, the lust that built to a frenzied climax was shared by both of us, savage in its way though anything but violent.

We lay quietly for a while, breathing hard but together, having run the same race. Then she slipped from under me and left me for a while, and I sat there stunned, managing only to think, *Well, nobody can say it wasn't consummated, can they?*

When she returned, she was in a pink satin robe with a rope sash and kitten-heel slippers. I'd managed to crawl back into my shorts, which took all I had left. She'd brought along a fluffy white blanket to spread down on the floor before the fire, which had settled into a subdued murmuring crackle, the once leaping flames now licking lazily. She sat on the blanket and lifted a feminine hand and bid me join her.

I did.

We nestled, her back to me, her lovely bottom pressed against me, a promise or perhaps a dare, as she held the hand of the arm I looped around her waist, and we slept.

I woke deep into the night.

She had rolled away a little, though was still on the white blanket, sleeping on her other side, breathing deep and gentle. I lifted her up and carried her in my arms, like a bride over a threshold, or maybe a monster lugging a distressed damsel. Either way, she didn't stir, wearing something like a smile on a mouth whose lipstick had all been used up.

In the bedroom, I tucked her in and she never roused. I thought about joining her but, oddly, that seemed a liberty I shouldn't yet take. I found my way to the john and got rid of some used beer, then trudged to the refrigerator for the fresh variety.

The fire had dwindled to glowing orange bits and pieces, but the warmth of the room remained. I sat in my boxers and sipped my Knickerbocker beer and reflected. Had I been bribed again? Paid off? I wasn't sure, and wasn't sure I cared. But I was an investigator by trade and inclination, and it didn't rub me right having so many questions still out there, unanswered.

Especially when among them was, *Who framed me for rape and murder?* As well as, *Who really did those crimes?* And, *Was I was looking for just one person?*

On the other hand, the answer to the first of those seemed obvious, just in case you think you're ahead of me.

That folksy benevolent monarch ruling from the Bluff, that smiling fish cannery magnate who hated the smell of his own wares, that welcoming future father-in-law so eagerly looking for a nobody like me to join the family business, was the only person with the kind of power in Killing Town to pull the various strings I was tangled up in.

The crunch of wheels on gravel, faint but easily discerned, caught my attention. I rose and moved through a room lit only by the meager glow of the moribund fire. At the front windows, I drew back a filmy curtain ever so slightly.

A car had pulled up.

Not right out front, down the road a ways, stopping in front of nowhere at all. With the night sky overcast and hiding any stars and moon, all I could make out was the vehicle's general dark hue—might be black or dark blue or a deep green. Nothing special, just a Chevy sedan with a New York license plate. Nothing special except for the guy who got out on the driver's side, and the other guy who climbed out on the rider's side.

The driver had the build of a heavyweight boxer, which he had once been. Even in the dim light, the oval of his face and its flat nose and thick lips were easy to make out, as was the sideways scar on his right cheek. Thick black eyebrows met in the middle and thinning widow's-peaked black hair was greased back, leaving bald streaks. He was in a dark suit with a dark tie and might have been a plainclothes dick or an insurance salesman. But he wasn't.

He was Tony Pigozzi.

The rider was short and fat with the same kind of dark suit and dark tie as his partner, but he wore a porkpie fedora, very sharp, which didn't help since he had the face of a pig with a mustache. No one would mistake him for a plainclothes dick or an insurance salesman.

He was Tony Scarnetti.

Those who enjoy irony might get a kick out of the Tony named Pigozzi having the scar, and the Tony named Scarnetti bearing the pig's puss. The hilarity of that, however, was lost on me at the moment.

The Two Tonys were heading toward the cottage, in no apparent rush. They might have been mailmen, though this was a peculiar time to make a delivery. Each had an automatic in his right hand, fairly good-size—.45s or nine millimeters, most likely. These were already raised and ready.

I went to the chair where my clothes and my hardware were stacked, got the .45 from its sling and the .38 from the ankle holster. Then I hustled to the bedroom, shook Melba awake, and told her wide-eyed face, "Get under the bed. Men with guns. Do it!"

I had to give her credit—she did that without a qualm or question.

But I had a question as she scooted under the log-wood bed: "You ever use a gun?"

She nodded.

I held out the .38 and she reached out and took it.

I said, "Anybody who isn't me or somebody you trust, use that on them."

I had a pair of slip-on sneakers in my suitcase and I got those on. Otherwise, I was just in my boxers, looking like some ring opponent of Pigozzi's back in his prime. Mismatched a little—I was more a light heavyweight.

Returning to the window, I found them pausing in the road, just beyond the Ford parked out front. Pigozzi, said to be the brains of the duo, was pointing toward the cottage. Then he nodded toward the back and headed that way at an easy lope.

Pig-faced Scarnetti did something that made me smile, which under the circumstances took some doing. He dropped his automatic—a Browning Hi-Power, I judged—in his right suitcoat pocket. Then he dug for something in an inside pocket and returned with a pouch about the size of an unfolded wallet. From this he selected what were almost certainly lock picks, smiled to himself, and started toward the front door, which I opened and shot him in the head.

He seemed to reflect on that, hanging there in space in the midst of blood mist, his two dark little eyes joined by a dark little hole between them. Then he flopped backward with a thud, the porkpie hat pushing down over the pig face, sparing the living from having to look at it.

Of course my shot had torn a big gaping hole in the silence, alerting Pigozzi, and I decided to head around the cottage after him rather than go through the house. I figured he wasn't inside, since I hadn't heard him bust the door down or anything, and if he'd been using lock picks, too, that gunshot had surely stopped that effort.

If I was wrong, and he was somehow already inside, I had to hope Melba really did know her way around a firearm. But me coming in behind him would be a break. Shooting an asshole in the back was a good way to end a gun fight before it got really ugly.

But when I came around, the back door was closed and the patio was empty. Pigozzi hadn't had time to pick that lock and get inside and close the door behind him; and he hadn't forced it open. I could see his Chevy parked down from here, but he wasn't heading to it. Maybe he'd tucked behind the garage… only then wouldn't he have taken a shot at me?

I checked anyway.

No sign of him there, but then I heard him, heard his footsteps as he ran, crunching twigs and leaves, batting branches out of his way as he went up that terribly steep, heavily wooded incline. That wall of green and brown, almost black in the night, showed no sign of him, as if it had swallowed him. But as he clawed and smashed through all that greenery, he created a percussive symphony that told of his fleeing.

I paused for just a moment.

I was damn near bare ass, in just the boxers and my sneakers, and heading through that thickness of brush and undergrowth, not to mention full-grown trees, I would get more scrapes and scratches than breaking up a pair of tom cats going at it over pussy.

But what choice did I have?

I glanced around to see if I could tell where exactly he'd taken off from, so I could take advantage of the path he'd forged. In the dark, with an area so wide, that was hopeless. The best I could do was follow the sounds.

"Shit," I muttered to nobody, and started up the incline, pushing through bushes and past low-lying trees, following the noise of him knifing through up ahead of me, protected by his goddamn suit of clothes, while nettles and thistles and prickly shrubs had their way with me, the nicks and cuts and even gashes already stinging. I pressed on, little blood trails making random patterns on my flesh, for thirty seconds that felt like thirty minutes.

Then the sound of him halted, and so did I.

Had he heard my pursuit, and stopped to lie in wait?

Nothing.

Nothing.

Nothing.

Then *something*, something I could hardly believe.

The sound said he was moving *toward* me! *Doubling back? Why?*

But he wasn't really—the crunch-crunch-crunch of twigs and leaves and branches being pushed aside had shifted, were now off to my left, growing louder at first, then less so.

In fact, moving away...

He was heading back to his car! He'd heard me in pursuit or thought he had, and decided to cut at an angle that would take him to the car parked alongside the road, down from the cottage. He was the driver— he had the keys. Not a dumb move, not a dumb move at all.

My choices were limited. I could cut toward him, hoping my progress through the brush and trees was quicker than his, although the angle he was taking made that doubtful. My only other option, and I could waste no time in choosing, was to double back myself. From the patio I would have a clear shot at the car or at him approaching it from the wooded hillside. He would have to cut in front of my path—at a distance, but in front of it.

I doubled back. After all, I'd scuffed and scraped my skin to hell and gone making a path—why not take it?

And the descent was definitely quicker and easier than the ascent. I could hear him, to my right now, still snapping and splintering his way through, the leaves he was disrupting rustling like a hundred birds heading for the sky from the safe haven of trees. He would be hearing much the same from me.

My ears told me he reached the clearing before I did, the ground taking a sudden gentle slope after the drastic descent he'd just maneuvered. That had to have slowed him down. Maybe he even stumbled. When I reached the garage, I held my palms out to brace me, then skirted the structure to get to the patio.

He was at the Chevy and getting in.

The shot I threw was wild and at this range hopeless. But the thunder of it was enough to freeze him. That scarred mug scowled at me as I came at him, still half a football field away, and instead of getting behind the wheel and taking off, and maybe shooting at me out his window, he planted himself on the gravel road and took aim.

He might have hit me if I hadn't anticipated the shot and rolled, grateful I was on grass not gravel. Then, instead of getting in the Chevy and the hell away, he came toward me, not even running, the .45 pointed in my direction but staying silent.

He'd misread it—I had rolled a fraction of a second after he fired, and he thought I'd been hit!

I was down on my side and I stayed put. Stayed motionless. The flat-nosed ex-pug was grinning down at me, so wide a grin the sideways scar turned into a second smile itself; he was ready to give me one last shot just for fun. He didn't know my unblinking open eyes were still seeing and when I swung my arm up and shot him in the head, he was still grinning.

He went backward, already dead and, despite his grin suggesting the contrary, unable to enjoy the red wet fireworks exploding from the top of his skull.

But I know I did.

CHAPTER TEN

The soggy gray blanket of the sky rumbled and grumbled as I dragged Pigozzi to the Chevy and got him up and in behind the wheel. Then I did the same with Scarnetti on the rider's side. It took some effort but my adrenalin was pumping, and I wasted no time. A guy in his boxers, all cut up and bleeding, hauling a couple of dead goons across the highway might have raised questions if someone drove by.

But no one did. This was damn near a private lane, this stretch of it anyway, and the other summer cottages along here were closed up for the coming cold.

I was pretty wiped out by the time I stumbled inside. I came in the front door and called out, *"Me!"* and went to her in the bedroom, the .45 in my hand but at my side now. She was still under the log-wood bed, her eyes glittering in the near-dark like a cornered animal's.

I flipped the light switch, said, "Me," again, then went over and knelt and held out a hand.

When she was on her feet, still in the pink satin robe but no slippers, she got her first look at me. Her eyes showed white all around, which went well with her gasp.

"Good lord, Mike—what *happened* to you?"

My body was a welter of welts and nicks and scrapes, blood dried now in odd little trails, making modern art out of me. Maybe they could hang me in a museum and people could stare and wonder what the hell I meant.

"Honey, I just killed two men."

She gasped again, but this time held it, and stood there stunned for several moments of suspended animation.

She was still that way when I asked, "Can you get your daddy on the phone?"

Looking numb now, she nodded, several times.

"Do it," I said. "I'll explain to him and you can listen."

The phone was on the wall in the kitchenette. She dialed. Took a while for her to get an answer, not surprising at half-past four in the morning.

"Daddy? It's Mel… No, I'm fine. I'm *fine*, but Mike needs to talk to you."

She handed me the receiver, like a cornered outlaw giving up a gun.

"Senator," I said, "I need your advice and maybe your help."

"Is my daughter all right?"

"She is. She's safe, a little rattled, but fine."

"What is this about, son?"

"It's about the real reason I came to Killington."

And I told him—and by doing so told them both—that I had sneaked into town to deliver some money to the wife of a recently deceased army buddy, who had entrusted the loot to me because it was hot even for hot money.

"This wasn't strictly legal, sir. My friend worked for a criminal outfit before the war, and that's who he stole it from. Somehow they got a line on me coming to town and two men came around tonight—how they knew where to find me I'm not sure—to try to collect that money and kill me. They would likely have killed your daughter as well, just because she was here."

An edge came into his voice. "You put my daughter in grave danger."

"Unintentional, sir. But the advice I need is this—what do I do with the bodies? They're sitting dead as hell in the car they came in, and it's parked just down the road. It was self-defense and I can sell that, but my track record with the local cops isn't great. Plus, I moved the bodies because I didn't figure you wanted them littering up your property. Maybe if you called it in and paved the way, I wouldn't get the rubber hose treatment or just flat-out shot."

He said nothing.

So I went on: "Or, since as you said, you're not without influence, maybe you'd like to clean up this mess for the sake of your daughter and her future husband."

He said nothing.

"I have a feeling," I said, "there's probably some road not so close to this one where a couple of goombahs who got bumped off in a mob dispute might turn up. Or a fishing boat that could maybe provide a couple burials at sea. Or a cliff where—"

"I'll take care of it."

There was nothing at all folksy or fatherly in that voice now.

"I would like," I said, "to bring your daughter to you. I think she would be safer with you than anywhere else in this city."

Melba, who had been taking this all in with a frown, her lips parted as if about to speak, finally did: "Mike, I have an apartment in town. There's no reason—"

But her father was talking and I lifted a palm to shush her.

"That's a good idea, Mike," he said, the friendly father-in-law tone returning somewhat. "I can put some staff on."

"I don't know if you're thinking of using any local cops," I said, "but I wouldn't. The only person I told where I was staying was Chief Belden."

"Belden can be trusted."

"I was of that opinion myself, but maybe it's loose lips sink ships. He must have mentioned my whereabouts to somebody in that stinking department. Somebody who can be bought and would know where to go to sell information."

"…I have security staff at the two plants. I'll enlist help from those ranks."

"Good. Look for us by dawn."

I hung up.

Melba, looking shell-shocked, stumbled over and started some coffee. I told her that was a good idea and went off to shower. I stripped out of my boxers, which were torn and streaked with green from the woods I'd plowed through, and got myself under the needles. I tried hot and that hurt, and cold and that hurt, too. Lukewarm felt fine, but when I soaped my scraped skin, it stung. I kept soaping.

I was toweling off when she slipped into the bathroom, which was barely big enough for us both. Her shell-shock was wearing off, replaced by concern as she took in my scratched-up body. Mostly they were superficial nothings, but a couple of the wounds were running blood again, their light scabbing scrubbed off in the shower.

She opened the medicine cabinet over the sink and got out a bottle of Mercurochrome and started daubing the nastier places a festive orange-red. It stung but the effort said she cared, and granted an implied forgiveness for me not sharing the truth with her earlier.

On the other hand, she still had plenty of truth yet to share with me.

I got back into my suit and packed my bag. She didn't pack anything, saying her father would have some things from her apartment sent over. We left the

Ford behind and I drove her to the Colonial mansion atop the Bluff, with very few words exchanged along the way. Again she sat hugging herself as if it were colder than it was, but she did not hug the passenger door. I sensed no hostility or fear in her.

But as I was taking the sloping driveway up toward the mansion, which was aglow in landscape lighting, she said, "You killed two men."

"I did."

"Did it bother you?"

"No. Them trying to kill me bothered me. And you'd have been a civilian casualty."

"You make it sound like war."

"It was. It is."

"Will they try again?"

"I don't know. If they reported back to the people who sent them, before they came calling... maybe."

I rolled up to the pillared porch. The Senator, in a gold robe with black satin lapels, sash and cuffs, emerged, looking vaguely like a foreign potentate. His son, in a black-and-red plaid robe, lurked behind him like he ought to have a palm leaf fan. Both wore somber expressions.

I got out, opened Melba's door, and walked her up. Appearing from behind Lawrence came Eva, like an ameba splitting off from itself. She was in a pale yellow chenille robe that hung on her like a lampshade; but even without make-up, her pretty features and tousled blondeness explained how Lawrence might have once come to marry her.

Eva moved quickly to Melba and put an arm around her and walked her inside, Lawrence following. Mel glanced at me just before she disappeared, her expression that of a kid dropped off at a new school.

The Senator and I were alone on the porch now, the patriarch's homely face working on inventing some brand-new wrinkles.

"I can use somewhere to stay," I said. "Suggestions?"

"I'll book you a room at the Killington Arms." Then he gave me a coldly accusatory stare. "Will any others come looking?"

I told him what I'd told Melba, but added, "Those two were the Mafia's top torpedoes in New York City. *Were.* The word will get out soon enough—tangle with Mike Hammer and catch a slug in the head or maybe in the back. They'll know I play it the same dirty way they do, and the ones who are smart will steer clear."

His eyes flared; nostrils, too. "Let us pray they are smart. Because I won't abide you putting my girl in any further danger."

"I don't intend to, but I live the life I live. Your family will have to put up with it. I'm going to assume you're aware that our upcoming vows are your daughter's idea. She got me out from under two very nasty criminal charges, and I appreciate that. And I like her."

His head came back and his eyelids rolled up. "You think you're doing her a *favor*, marrying her?"

I grinned at him. "I don't know. What do you think?"

And with the sun filtering through the maple trees surrounding the mansion of the town's number one mover-and-shaker, I got in my fiancée's Packard and drove off to find myself a diner.

I'd had a busy night and could use some breakfast.

The house was something a realtor would call Colonial, but had nothing in common with the Colonial the Senator and his family lived in. This was just a modest one-and-a-half-story bungalow, white with dark green shutters, a walk winding up a small front yard dressed up with a handful of house-hugging bushes, a one-car garage off to the right.

Nothing much.

Just the life guys like Bob Lewis fought for overseas. Just the home front dream of wife and kids and a decent roof over your head.

I went up three cement steps to the stoop, looking like a prosperous door-to-door salesman in the fresh suit and tie I'd got into in my new hotel room. It was nine a.m. At the door, I knocked hard, because I heard a sweeper going.

It shut off and she answered quickly, impressive when you saw how pregnant she was. Her maternity top was floral, pink and white and yellow, her slacks dark blue, her sandals mustard-colored. Her hair was in a black-and-yellow bandana and she wore not a speck of make-up. But like Eva this morning, she was a beauty.

Big wide-set baby-blue eyes with long curled-up lashes, a cute little nose, generous full lips, apple cheeks and a complexion like the cream you pour on strawberries.

The guys must have been lining up to make a mother out of this babe, but Bob had the lucky ticket. He'd always been a lucky son of a buck. Almost always.

"Yes?" she said, giving me a smile I hadn't earned, her voice high and a little breathy.

"Mrs. Loomis?"

"Yes?"

"I'm Mike Hammer. A friend of Bob's."

Her eyes lit up. "Yes! Bob spoke of you often. Come in, come in! Please, come in."

The living room, like the house itself, was modest but attractive. A couch and a couple of end tables and a matching chair were enough to fill the small area, with that Hoover in its midst. A little table had pictures of Bob and my hostess, and some other family photos. She scurried the vacuum clear out of the room, despite my protests, and wouldn't hear of it till I'd agreed to coffee.

We had that in a full kitchen a little bigger than the cottage's kitchenette. Everything was white and new, wedding gifts most likely. She sat me at a yellow-and-white Formica-topped table and served up coffee in jadeite cups, then excused herself to go to the bathroom. She smiled, a little embarrassed, and said, "Comes with the territory," and I grinned.

When she returned, I had my coffee with a little cream and she took both cream and sugar. That she'd been doing some crying was clear, but Bob had been gone for over a week, so my guess was it was mostly happening at night now.

I began, "Mrs. Loomis—"

"Make it Mitzi, Mr. Hammer. Mike?"

"Mike."

"And we both know my name isn't really Loomis, although, well… I believe I may eventually have it changed, legally. Assuming I can get my job back at the cannery."

"You're a local girl?"

She nodded. "Yes, and my folks still live here, so my mom will play babysitter. Bob had a really good job at the fish-glue factory. He was on his way to foreman. I wish… I wish he could have been more patient."

Something prickled at the back of my neck.

"How do you mean?" I asked, although I was afraid I already knew.

The lovely face gave me the saddest, sweetest smile you ever saw. "Mike… I know about what Bob did. How he died. His brother Bill—who I've never met—called and said Bob died 'suddenly in his sleep.' That Bob had heart trouble since childhood that he never told me about."

"But you already knew Bob was gone, and about—"

"The robbery? The shooting? Yes. A girl friend of mine from here got a job a few months ago in Brooklyn, and she saw it in the papers and called me."

"How did Bob's brother keep you away from the funeral?"

Her shrug was barely perceptible. "Well, it was already over by the time he called. He said Bob's folks preferred I stay away. I'm Baptist and Bob was Catholic, and his people didn't want anything to do with me. That much was true, when he was alive. How they feel now, I have no idea."

I leaned an elbow on the Formica, gestured with an open hand. "I understand they passed the hat for you. Family and friends, they really came through." I got out the packet of thousand dollar bills and tossed it on the kitchen table between us, like a poker bet.

I lost.

"I know where that's from," she said, staring at it expressionlessly, the baby-blues unblinking. "Bob didn't lie to me about his past. I know he was involved with those Mafia people. He did bad things before I met him. Not terrible things, maybe, but bad enough. And I didn't care, as long as that part of his life was over. We started a new life here."

Seemed to me that there were better places to live than Killington, but what the hell—everybody has to live somewhere.

She leaned forward a little, just a little, because that's all she could manage. She tapped the envelope with a forefinger. "I know what this is. I don't know how much it is, but I'm going to guess quite a lot."

"It's twenty-nine thousand dollars," I said.

She blinked.

I went on: "I kept out a thousand for the job and expenses. Bob was insistent about that."

She frowned, curious. "I thought you were a policeman. Didn't you always want to be a policeman?"

I grinned at her. "Well, at first I wanted to be a numbers runner. But I came around. Anyway, I'm a private detective now. And this is a job I'm doing for Bob. If you don't want to keep the money, that's up to you. I don't want anything more to do with it."

"It's stolen money. You could turn it in."

"It's off-the-books money. Dirty money being cleaned through a front business. And the one thing I won't do for you, Mitzi, is give that money back to those crumbs."

She smiled. "He wrote about you."

"In V-mail, you mean?"

She nodded. "He wrote about a lot of the fellas he served with. But he really liked you. He said you were very brave but a little crazy."

"He had that backwards."

She liked that. Wow, could this dame work up a smile. We drank coffee.

"So you would suggest I take it," she said.

"No."

"No?"

"No. I insist."

She laughed a little. "What would I do with it?"

"Is this house free and clear?"

"Heavens no!"

"How did Bob afford it?"

"He got a loan. The bank here is very cooperative with factory workers who get a high approval rating from the Old Man."

That was how Lawrence had referred to his father.

"The Senator, you mean?"

She nodded. "He's good to his workers. Pays them well. Bit of a windbag and full of himself, but that…"

"Comes with the territory?"

Another nod.

"So, Mitzi—how much do you owe on this place?"

"Four thousand."

"That will leave twenty-five thousand. How much do you make a year, when you're at the cannery?"

"Two thousand."

"So take a couple years off and be a mom. The cannery will survive. Call it four grand. That leaves twenty-one thousand. You drive a new car?"

"Don't be silly. But what I have gets me around."

"What is it?"

"A beat-up old Nash."

"Call it two thousand for a new Oldsmobile with all the trimmings. Live a little."

Her lips pursed in amusement. "Won't all that be a little bit conspicuous?"

"Do it gradually. Pay the house off, wait a year, buy the car. Do you have a nursery decked out?"

"No. Why do that till I know what I have?"

"Well, it'll be a baby."

"Yes, but a boy or a girl?"

"Probably."

She laughed. "Bob said you were funny."

"Did he?"

"In particular, a master of the off-color joke."

"Well, you'll have to take Bob's word for that. Telling an expectant mother about a farmer's daughter just seems wrong somehow."

We both laughed a little.

I stood. "Well, I have things to do."

"Having to do with the Charles girl?"

That blindsided me. "Pardon?"

"Sit down, Mike. Have another cup of coffee."

I sat and had one. "You know about the... jam I got in?"

"Everyone in town knows about it. They might not recognize you, as I didn't at first, because those weren't exactly... flattering photos the papers ran. But your name's on everyone's lips. Not everyone comes to town on a freight, gets indicted for rape and murder, and then winds up in the society column with the woman who cleared him."

"That sums it up nicely."

"I knew the Warburton girl a little. The Old Man is something of a rake, and his son isn't much better. She was a flirt who wound all the men in that cannery around her little finger, and finally wound up in the office."

I frowned. "Was she having an affair with one of them?"

"That I can't tell you. Wouldn't be surprised. Tell me something, Mike."

"Okay."

"Why hop a freight? They have trains you can catch in New York, I understand. And a bus or two."

She had a right to know. I really should have told her already, but I didn't want to discourage her about the money.

"Sneaking into Killington made sense," I said. "The people Bob liberated that dough from know I was a friend of his. And word got out I visited him in that hospital shortly before he passed."

"Am I in any danger?"

Should I tell her how I got the nicks and scrapes on my face, or just let her figure the local cops did that?

"You might be," I said. "Whether you accept your husband's money or not. If they somehow track you down, you could be in danger, yes. That's something else to spend some money on—a gun."

"Bob covered his tracks well when he came to town."

"I'm sure he did. But two men found out I was in Killington—I may have sneaked in, but trouble found me just the same. Like you said, I made the papers."

"What about the two men?"

"They're not a problem now. Possibly someone else knows what they found out, but I'll deal with that, too. It should have no bearing on the money."

The blue eyes saucered. "Well, of course it has a bearing on the money!"

"Mitzi—Bob wanted you to have it. He wanted his kid to have it. He gave his life getting it."

"But it was a stupid thing to do what he did. A crazy, stupid thing!"

"But he did do it. For you." I nodded to the bulge beneath the smock. "And him, or her."

I got up. She started to rise, but I motioned her not to. "You just finish your coffee. I'll find my way out."

She nodded. Her eyes were on the packet.

"You need to tell me you're taking it," I said. "Even if you drop it in the collection plate at the First Baptist Church. Mail that thing back to me, and I'll be on your doorstep again, shoving it at you."

Her face was all screwed up with doubt. "You think… you *really* think it's the right thing to do?"

I shrugged. "It's the thing Bob wants you to do."

She swallowed, reached for the packet, pressed it to her bosom. "Thank you, Mike."

"Don't thank me. Thank Bob."

And I went back out to the Packard, good deed done.

By all rights, I should take the train back to Manhattan, this time with a ticket and a seat. Only I still had business in Killing Town.

CHAPTER ELEVEN

I headed back to the Killington Arms hotel, which wasn't the Ritz but was a big step up from the near-flophouse I'd checked into on my first night in town. The room was well-appointed, clean and comfortable, and I closed the curtains, stripped down to my skivvies and flopped on top of the covers.

A couple of hours was all I needed to make up for the beauty sleep the Two Tonys interrupted. I rolled out of the rack refreshed, went and splashed water on my face, and got back into my suit, tie, raincoat, and hat, with the .45 and .38 snugged in their respective homes.

I was ready to make mischief.

The dingy hash house run by a bald little wop named Lonnie Shaker wasn't jumping, not at three o'clock on a Saturday afternoon. Lonnie wasn't around, but the green-eyed waitress with the black-streaked blonde hair was waiting tables, or would be if somebody walked in.

I took a corner booth. Her back was to me, her slender frame with the nice fanny taking up a stool at the counter, where she was loafing and sucking on a smoke till a customer came in. And I qualified, so she spun around, ditched the cig, climbed off the stool and walked over with the enthusiasm of a taxi dancer at the end of a long shift.

She didn't recognize me. Hell, she didn't look at me, her eyes on her order pad, her pencil ready. "What'll you have, bud?"

Not very original.

Nor was my response: "Why don't you take a load off, sugar?"

Lifting her chin so that her eyes could take me in seemed like a job she was barely up to. But she did it. Then those eyes, those pretty green eyes, flared. She backed away a step.

"I… I don't want any trouble," she said.

I showed her the sawbuck. "No hard feelings. Just a little conversation."

She shook her head, looking around, as if ghosts at the empty tables littering the joint might be eavesdropping.

"He has a little finif brother," I said, with a nod to the ten-spot. "Be a shame to break up a happy family."

Her brow furrowed and she got less pretty. "Do you know the kind of trouble you could get me in?"

"The cops aren't interested in me anymore, doll. I'm in the clear. Just curious about a few things. Your boss around?"

"Lonnie's in back."

"Tell him you're taking a ten-minute break. Get us both some coffee and come back and get comfy. We're about to make friends again."

She frowned in thought, then nodded, and did all that.

Across the booth from me now, she was pouring sugar into her coffee. I put some cream in mine.

"Did they do that to you?" she asked, wiggling a finger at my face, chipped red polish on its nail.

"No. I took a walk in the woods."

"You can get poison ivy doing that."

"There's worse things a guy can catch. Really, I just have one question, and maybe a follow-up or two."

She glanced at the ten. Shrugged. "Okay."

"Who approached you? Who arranged the frame?"

"What frame?"

"Let's skip that, sister. You want the tenner, you got to play for my team. Who set me up?"

She snorted a laugh. "Who do you think? Who is it *always*?"

"I'm a stranger in town, remember. Help me out here."

"Sykes." She giggled. "I hear you put him in the hospital."

"Yeah. You may recall, I was kicking a field goal and his balls got in the way."

She almost spit out a mouthful of coffee. She swallowed and said, "They say... they say he got hauled in with two and came out with one. You know, ball? Testi-what's-it?"

"Testicle. I heard that. You suppose he holds a grudge?"

Overly plucked eyebrows rose. "Kind of amazing you're still alive, mister. Sykes is kind of the... *other* police chief around this burg. That Belden character, he's no crook. No saint, but no crook. Sykes fixes the fixes, frames the frames, and every bent cop in town kicks back a piece of their action."

I slid the ten over to her. "Thanks, honey."

"What happened to his little brother?"

"I have one other question and it may be harder. You may have to settle for the Alexander Hamilton."

"Who?"

I tapped on the face on the bill. "Somebody who got shot. You weren't the only one who fingered me, kid."

"I didn't finger you. I said I didn't remember you. That's different."

"Not when a cop puts on wet leather gloves and plays slap and tickle with me, it isn't. They rounded up a little guy who did identify me. Little dipso. Any chance you know who that would be?"

She nodded. "That's one of Sykes' favorite witnesses. Eddie Something. Sykes uses him all the time. But word is he hopped a freight after you got sprung. I heard he was afraid you might come lookin' for him."

She shrugged. "Isn't that what you're doing now?"

I admitted it was. And the irony of Eddie hopping a freight to escape my attentions wasn't lost on me.

I got out the engraving of another guy who got shot and tossed it to her, and she brightened and said thanks, then told me she'd take care of the coffee. On the house!

But I bet Lonnie didn't know.

The cellar bar where the cops had caught up with me was doing better business than the hash house, but just barely. I knew it was a long shot the brunette would be there. Too early, and she hadn't seemed to be a regular—more like she was slumming on a slow night. But I had to try.

No luck.

I tried six other gin mills of varying standards.

No luck there, either.

But that's the funny thing about luck—you never know when it'll tap you on the shoulder. Back at my hotel, I stopped in at the cocktail lounge for a highball. I sat at the bar and nursed it, thinking about my next move, when the brunette I'd been looking for settled in on the stool next to me. Didn't tap me on the shoulder exactly, but close enough.

She didn't see me at first, or at least I don't think she did. She was in a sexy red satin off-the-shoulder number with a V neckline. V for victory, if you had the loot.

She said to the bartender, "Whiskey and ginger."

I said, "Make it Scotch. Best you got. Soda on the side." Like before.

All that hair bounced as she turned to me with a lovely smile, not so professional this time. "Don't tell me this is that better time and better place?"

"It'll do till the real thing comes along. Shall we?"

I collected my drink and nodded to the bartender to have hers brought over and we took a corner booth, black leather, button-tufted. A fancy framed black panther picture hovered. This was more than a step up from the cellar bar.

"I've been following you," she said, "in the papers."

"You make me sound like a comic strip."

"You get those scratches from our friendly local gendarmes?"

"No. This is from an ill-advised outing. The swelling the cops gave my baby face finally came down, but I have a good memory."

She leaned forward, previewing the goodies. "I just bet you do."

"Did you know I was looking for you?"

"No! Be still my heart. Rumor is you got a girl. Rich. Beautiful. What do you need with me?"

"I'm sure we could think of something. But what I'm really after is information. When somebody frames me for rape and murder, I take it personal. Kind of want to do something about it."

"I can see that." She got a deck of Chesterfields

out of her little red clutch purse and made a selection. "But how could I be of any help on that score?"

I gave her light from a matchbook. "You *know* this town. You work in it. Your line of endeavor takes grease. And before that you did time in the cannery. You know things an out-of-towner wouldn't. For example—what can you tell me about this Sykes character?"

She shrugged, let out an "o" of smoke through a red lipstick portal. "He's the top crooked cop in town. What else do you need to know about him? If you were framed—and you *were* framed, right?—he either did it or gave it his stamp of approval."

"Yeah. I had his stamp of approval, all right."

"I really don't know any more about him than that. I never dealt directly with him. Sorry."

"That's okay, kid. What about the Warburton girl?"

That threw her a little. "What about her?"

"Did you know her? Was she a working girl?"

She shook her head, but said, "I knew her a little, only she never hooked that I know of. Not that she didn't have the makings and the… inclination."

"How did you know her?"

"Well, *where* I knew her was at the cannery. She could play the guys above her like cheap kazoos. She started on the line, but wound up in the office. She was the Senator's secretary for a while. Then she got transferred over to the fish-glue factory, where she was the Senator's son's gal Friday."

"Both the father and the son had her as—"

"Leave it right there. Both the father and the son had her. You have to understand, the Charles men are shameless letches."

"Did you ever have them as clients?"

"No. But after Jean Warburton went over to the fish-glue plant, to be Junior's secretary, I became the Senator's *new* secretary. And he wanted for free what I value dearly."

I leaned toward her. "The *Senator* was the boss with busy hands? The one you clubbed with an ashtray?"

She laughed some smoke out. "The very captain of industry himself, the old—what's the fancy word?— satyr. And sonny boy, they say, is no better. So, uh… Mike, right?"

"Right."

"Don't you have any bad habits *you'd* like to indulge? Wouldn't cost you a thing, although I wouldn't frown at a gratuity."

"Sorry, honey. I'm spoken for."

"It's really true, then? You're going to marry that poor little rich girl? She *is* a fetching thing."

"You aren't hard to look at, either. Buy you another drink?"

She shook the brunette mane. "No thanks. I'm working and have to gauge my intake. Look me up sometime, Mike, on my off hours… after you've been married a while."

She slid out of the booth, then leaned in and gave me a sticky little kiss. Then she swayed over and found herself a stool at the bar.

And me with a room in this hotel.

I finished my highball and went up to it.

I called the *Herald* and asked the switchboard girl for Mort Jackson, a reporter who had covered my arrest, the coroner's jury, and even that farce at the police station when Melba got me shaken loose.

"Jackson, City Desk," a rushed voice said over the typewriter clatter, muffled talk and general newsroom bustle.

"Mike Hammer, Mr. Jackson."

That got his attention, but after a couple of seconds he said, dismissively, "I coulda used an interview a couple days ago, Hammer. Now you're what we call old news, my friend. And I'm on deadline for the morning edition."

"I'll meet you when you've turned your copy in," I told him. "It'll be worth your time. I can tell you all about how the Senator and his family reacted to having a freight-hopper for a son-in-law."

He took another couple seconds to chew that, then said, "Dingbat's, around the corner on Broadway and Ninth. Hour from now."

He clicked off.

Dingbat's was a hangout for reporters, a hole in the wall but more respectable than the other dives I'd sampled in town. The walls were decorated with framed front pages—PROHIBITION ENDS AT LAST!, HINDENBURG

EXPLODES!, U.S. DECLARES WAR!, that kind of thing. The only women present, always in the company of two or more men, were hard-looking news hens adding to the fog of cigarette smoke. Beer and the occasional boilermaker seemed the libations of choice.

I found a back booth, ordered a beer and got a Lucky going. Why not add to the atmosphere? I was on a second beer when he finally came in, twenty after eleven.

"Last minute rewrite," Jackson said, a little guy in a rumpled off-the-rack suit, loose tie, and shapeless hat, a cigarette bobbing in thin lips. He had the typically anonymous look of a good reporter, but if you paid attention, the small dark eyes were alert—even at the end of a long day. Unbidden, a waitress delivered a glass of beer and he thanked her with a wink.

With no further social niceties, he dug a spiral pad and a pencil out of his pocket and said, "So I bet you went over real big with the Senator and the assorted Charleses."

"That's what makes it interesting," I said.

"What does?"

"I got a ticker tape parade out of 'em. Of course, I'm not the hobo you guys made me out to be. If I wasn't old news, maybe you'd have dug a little, like the Senator, and found out I have a distinguished war record, including not getting killed, am an ex-cop and currently a licensed private investigator out of Manhattan."

He pushed the pad away, tossed the pencil on it and looked at me closer. "This starts to interest me. I don't understand it, but it interests me."

I shrugged. "What interests me is that I'm still a stranger to everybody but Melba Charles, who met me at a USO dance during the war." I had to stick by that story, at least for now.

He was nodding a little. "Well, *there's* an angle, anyway. More like sob sister stuff, but sentimental crap with a wartime slant always plays. You had a long-distance romance, huh? Letters and stuff. You in a foxhole, her at the beauty shop?"

"You're missing the point. I'm a nobody to the most important family in town, and yet they take me in like Rockefeller, Jr. Why?"

His eyebrows hiked damn near to his crumpled hat brim. "Do I know?"

"I'm not sure *I* do. But somebody in that family is covering something up. I'm convinced the Senator framed me, or if his son did, it had to be with the old man's consent. Maybe guidance."

The sharp little eyes peered out of slits. "That's not a story, Hammer. That's opinion. I don't handle the editorial page. And if I did, I sure as hell wouldn't take on Senator Charles."

"You in his pocket, too?"

He smirked, pawed the air. "The *town's* in his pocket. You've been around here long enough to pick up on that. But if he framed you, why send his daughter to help you squirm your way out?"

"I was hoping you might know."

He thought for a moment. "I just might. You tangled with Sykes. You put him in a hospital bed. You have any idea of just how powerful he is in this town?"

"I'm starting to. Is he the Senator's boy?"

He shook his head. "That's not how it works, not in a town this size. Sykes is the guy in the department who the Senator goes to if there's a problem. In fairness to the old boy, I can't say it's a privilege he's ever abused. He's decent enough, for a guy with that kind of money and power."

"If you say so."

He leaned forward, eyes glittering. "But Sykes is the boy anybody who wants something done around here can go to—Mafia types who want to run whores or gambling, wealthy guys in Dutch, nice girls in trouble, respectable types who got caught in a bus station john with a John. It's quite a menu."

So that was how the Two Tonys found me—Sykes had led them to me. Even if the "Mafia types" were local, they'd have New York City ties.

"If Sykes went off the deep end and flat-out murdered you in custody," Jackson said, "think of the unwanted attention it would attract. The Senator might have gone to great lengths to tamp that down."

"What's the score on Belden?" I asked, figuring Sykes could only have got my location through him.

"He's as straight as possible in a town like this."

"Which doesn't sound all that straight. Would he pass information to Sykes?"

He shook his head again. "I don't think so. Anyway, not intentionally. But a chief of police can be isolated from the rank and file. He could pass something on through an intermediary to Sykes without even knowing."

"He's that naive?"

"No. He's in that corrupt a department. Do I have to tell you they're a bunch of bully boys?"

"They already made that point, thanks. So what do you know about the Warburton girl?"

He shrugged. "I know her brothers are low-class trash and maybe so was she, but at least she had ambition. She was trying to better herself... working with what she had."

"And I guess we both know what she had. You want to tell me about how she and the Senator and his son tie up?"

He almost flinched at that, and his kind of newshound doesn't flinch so easy. He waved the waitress over for another beer. I was still working on my second one.

He took a few sips.

I had all night. I could wait.

Then he said, "The way this works is, I ask you questions. You're not supposed to pump me."

"Did you sleep through the part where I said I was an investigator? I'm going to find out what's going on with that girl's rape and murder. And it's going to make a hell of a story."

"...If I can print it."

"And why wouldn't you be able to?" I gave him a nasty grin. "Would it have anything to do with the Warburton girl being the Senator's pink-collar plaything at the cannery? And after that went on to be his son's secretary at the fish-glue factory?"

He waved the idea off. "There's nothing to that."

"Why not?"

He snorted a laugh. "Those two are a couple of chasers from way back, and everybody in this town knows it. The Senator's a dirty old man. And like father, like son... And when either one gets tired of the latest model, he pays her off and sends 'er packing. Enough hush money can heal all sorts of hurt feelings, y'know. That pair doesn't have to do any more than that, even if they are—"

"Lady killers?"

He leaned forward, keeping his voice low. "Look, Old Man Charles is more king than senator. He can do what he wants in his kingdom. Still, he's paid dearly over the years, for being on the make, and in a lot of ways."

"Such as?"

"Well... everybody says he loved his late wife, but he couldn't control his urges, and look how *that* turned out."

"How did it turn out?"

"You didn't know? She killed herself. Cut her wrists in the bathtub."

"Hell. When was this?"

"Long time ago. Twenty years?"

When Melba was just nine.

"The real creep in the family," the reporter went on, "is that son of his. *Lawrence.*" He said the name like it was a dirty word. "Larry married that sweet wife of his, back when she was a real beauty. She was a runner-up for Miss Rhode Island in Miss America, you know."

"I didn't know."

"They say Lawrence was faithful, as far as she knew, for a time. But after she had her first kid, she blew up like a balloon. Second kid, she went dirigible."

HINDENBURG EXPLODES!

"Bastard doesn't even bother hiding his tomcatting from her," Jackson said. "And look at how they both behave! The father thinks Miss Warburton is getting too close for comfort, she's talking marriage and God knows what she has to hang over the old S.O.B., so he shunts her off to his baby boy for sloppy seconds. '*You keep her happy, sonny.*'"

Then the Senator promoted another girl off the line, that brunette who as it turned out would rather turn tricks than put up with the slimy likes of the boss man.

Jackson was shaking his head, his expression disgusted in that worldly way reporters have. "They don't kill these girls, Hammer. Like I said—they pay them off, send them away, when they're tired of them, or feel threatened by talk of love and marriage, or, in Lawrence's case, divorce. Murder them? They just don't *have* to!"

"But it does explain why a hasty frame was arranged for me," I said. "Even if they had nothing to do with the girl's death, the Charles men would want that case closed up good and tight and right away, before their dirty laundry started smelling worse than their damn factories."

The reporter nodded. "Even in this town, you can't cover up something like that. Murder. Rape. But why would either of them rape that girl? Makes no sense."

I tossed a couple bucks on the table and slid out of the booth. "Thanks."

He frowned up at me. "So where's the story?"

"I'll give it to you," I said, "when I know what it is."

Out on the street, I lit up another Lucky. The overcast sky hadn't kept its promise. The sky was clear tonight, stars, moon, a full one at that. The works. The night was cool and pleasant, and while I hadn't assembled the puzzle yet, I was pretty sure I had all the pieces.

Somebody tapped me on the shoulder.

I wheeled and it was Sykes. The tall slender detective was in a raincoat and a derby. He cast his almost pretty, light-blue eyes on me, two nice jewels in the bony, angular setting that was his face.

"I hear you been askin' around about me," he said.

And somebody else tapped me.

Not on the shoulder.

CHAPTER TWELVE

The warehouse was close to the water, if my nostrils were to be believed—twitching with that familiar fishy stench that so defined Killington. The ceiling was high, crisscrossed with pipes from which occasional conical lamps hung like Asian rice hats, throwing amber spotlights as if some singer or dancer might come from the wings and start a vaudeville routine.

The floor was concrete and fairly clean, but the structure had been here a long time—it was a brick building with high, many-paned windows whose opaque glass let minimal illumination in, particularly now, at night, when street lamps were about it. Cardboard cartons were stacked ten feet high and six feet wide, forming aisles that wheeled carts could be conveyed down for loading. Some ladders on wheels were here and there, too. A few of the aisles were formed with wooden crates, similarly stacked, each box labeled CHARLES & COMPANY FISH GLUE. All very neat, and not terribly ominous. Just a place where men labored hard at dull necessary work.

But the only men working here tonight, both from the local police department, wouldn't have to work very hard, though it would probably not prove dull for them, if necessary in their view.

I was centerstage in the only open area, with double garage doors fore and a workbench aft, hanging by my wrists about two feet off the ground, like a beef carcass in a butcher shop. My shirt was off. The rope chewing into my wrists disappeared up into the rafters, tied off at an angle to my left. I was a solo performer featured in a yellow spotlight under one of those lamp-shade cones in the rafters.

My police department audience was Lieutenant Henry Sykes, still in his raincoat and derby and leather gloves, and that dish-faced, fat-bellied cop, wearing his blue uniform with shiny brass buttons like this was typical duty in Killing Town. Hell, maybe it was. His right shirtsleeve had been rolled up to accommodate the cast over his broken arm.

Sitting back on a couple of folding chairs, facing each other, the two men were drinking beer—a metal tub filled with cans of Rheingold between them—and laughing and talking. They were smoking cigars, too, like a couple of backroom politicians. I got the feeling they were waiting for me to come around and join the party.

And I had come around, just now, but within seconds I slitted my eyes near shut and kept my chin down against my chest. But I wasn't missing anything. They hadn't started beating me yet, but with these two, that would be coming. And since Sykes had gone to the hospital with two balls and come out with one—thanks to me—what awaited the third guest at the party was *not* likely to be a cold can of Rheingold and a cigar…

My muscles were aching like hell, my weight stretching my tendons like the rubber bands they weren't. I couldn't have been like this long, though—I still had feeling in my fingers, my hands, and that would go soon enough. And the back of my head where I'd been sapped was still wet with blood, not scabbed or dried yet. I was already having trouble breathing—this was damn near crucifixion, when your lungs got compressed to where you couldn't breathe. It wasn't the nails and infection and bugs or even the Romans that killed the religious martyrs— they suffocated. But at least my wrists and shoulders weren't dislocated yet.

Better yet, as I took this inventory, I realized I could still feel the little holster strapped in place on my right ankle under my trousers, with a heaviness that suggested the .38 was still there. They hadn't given me enough of a frisk, or felt it when they trussed me up, to tumble to it.

Dish Face said, "When are the New York guys coming over?"

The long-faced plainclothes dick checked his watch. "They had a couple of girls in their room. Said it would be half an hour, forty-five minutes."

"Gives us time to have some fun first."

Sykes shook his head. "They don't want us to kill him. He knows something they want to know."

The fat cop grunted in displeasure. "What are they after, out of him?"

"I don't know. Something to do with those other heavies we sent out to the Charles girl's cottage."

They each had some beer.

Then Dish Face asked, "You really think Hammer killed them both?"

"Why, you think they were playing Russian roulette, Sarge?"

The fat cop frowned over at me. "I mean, Jesus! He's *hanging* right there! Low hanging damn fruit! We're just gonna sit here and wait for somebody *else* to take over?"

Now Sykes glanced my way. "Well, we can offer to do the softening up for 'em. Just kind of throw that in for the five C's. I mean, we both got scores to settle with the son of a bitch."

Dish Face was damn near whining now. "Damnit, Henny, let's get started! Go wet down your gloves if you like. All we got to do is not kill him."

"…I suppose a little fun isn't going to hurt anybody."

"Anybody but *Hammer*!" And the fat prick started in on an *uh-haw, uh-haw* horse laugh.

Nothing from Sykes for a while.

Then: "Well… let's indulge ourselves a little."

Sykes pitched his cigar and rose, that tall frame of his unfolding like a circus guy on stilts. Dish Face did the same, only he didn't unfold—he more spilled out of his chair. In his left hand he was clutching a nightstick as straight and taut as he wasn't, a leather strap hanging like the tail of a beast.

Then they were standing in front of me, looking up at me like they had front row seats at a lynch party.

Disappointment dripped off Dish Face's voice. "Hell, he's still out. Where's the fun in that? Beatin' on a guy already out cold."

Sykes was staring up at me. "He isn't out. He's faking."

"You think so?"

"I think so. Give him a few love taps."

The fat cop swung the nightstick into my side. I didn't react. It hurt, but he'd missed my ribs, and with a lefthand swing—I'd put his right arm out of commission, remember—he didn't have all that much power.

But he did better with the second swing, and just great with the third, the snap of a rib damn near echoing in that big space.

Me, I just hung there, not giving them any satisfaction or excuse for another blow.

"I still say he's playing possum," Sykes said. "Let's see if he can bluff his way through *this*."

And Sykes gave me what he'd be saving up: a hard fist to the balls.

The hurt came in waves—searing pain followed by an instant throbbing headache, and the rush of nausea. Together, they made me bend over and cry out. It rang and echoed through the big, high-ceilinged chamber.

Sykes held his fat pal back with a thoughtful hand. "Keep cool, Sergeant. He might puke. You want that on your uniform? Give him time to compose himself."

I was breathing hard, experiencing a symphony of nausea and pain. But at least getting hit in the nuts did distract me from how much my arms and shoulders hurt.

Removing his restraining hand, Sykes said to the sergeant, "Now he should be fine."

Fat lips in a fat, concave face peeled back over crooked yellow teeth, and he barreled toward me, raising that nightstick high, like he was going to splatter the biggest damn cockroach anybody ever saw.

I raised my left foot and kicked out, giving him the flat of my Florsheim, making that stupid face even more concave.

He was on the floor, spitting bloody soup with a crouton of a tooth floating in it. Sykes, frowning in a *tsk-tsk* school-teacherly way, helped him up, saying, "Try again. I'll hold his legs."

Fat boy wiped the blood off his furious face and raised his nightstick, waiting for Sykes to restrain me. Before that could happen, I made a remark.

"Thirty grand," I said.

They both froze, looking up at me like hicks who just spotted a flying saucer in a swamp.

Sykes pushed Dish Face back a ways, straightened and managed to look down his nose at me despite our relative positions. "What was that you said?"

My turn to sneer. "These New York boys. They want to question me, between screwing B-girls and giving you a lousy five C's. Do you know why?"

Dish Face spluttered, "'Cause you killed two of theirs!"

"No," I said. I grinned down at them. "I'm sure they're not thrilled about that. But no, they want me to tell them where the thirty grand is."

Silence, broken only by a drip of water from some distant sink.

Then, quietly, Sykes asked, "What thirty grand?"

I said, "The thirty grand one of 'theirs' stole from them."

I didn't know how much they knew.

Well, Dish Face only knew they were doing a job for the New York Mafia. Sykes was another story. But he obviously didn't know about the money. So he must not have known much.

Sykes stepped closer, those blue eyes gazing up at me with pinpoint intensity. "*You* have it?"

"I know where it is."

"Are you the one who stole it?"

"No. A friend of mine did. Old army buddy. He sent me here with it, to give to his family."

"What's his name?"

I nodded toward the rope I was dangling from, as if maybe Sykes hadn't noticed it. "Get me down from here and we'll talk."

Dish Face shouted, "*No!*" and it rang off the rafters.

"Quiet," Sykes said, as if shushing a child. To me: "What do you have in mind?"

"Three-way split. Ten grand each."

Dish Face was grinning but there was no glee in it. "Yeah, and what do we do about those *New York* boys?"

If I hadn't been hanging from a rope, I'd have shrugged. "Kill them."

Dish Face, shaking his head so hard I was surprised it didn't rattle, turned to Sykes. "He's crazy! *You're* crazy!"

But Sykes was thinking it over, the pretty eyes in the long cadaverous face slitted in contemplation. "And who gets the blame, Hammer?"

"Me. I slip out of town, you slip ten grand each in your pockets, and dump the hoods wherever you like. Dealer's choice. I ain't choosy."

Sykes gave me a wide, thin smile as he peered up at me. "And they come after *you*, not us?"

"Right. Only I'm long gone. Me and my ten gees find some friendlier state to steal in."

Sykes turned to his sergeant. "Get him down."

Dish Face looked like he might bust out crying. "Are you *sure* about this, Henny?"

"Get him down. Leave his wrists tied and put him in a chair."

The fat cop let me down hard, figuring maybe I'd hurt myself, but I wasn't that far off the floor. Still, Sykes seemed rather impressed that I stayed on my feet and didn't tumble to the cement.

Now it could get tricky. If they tied my feet to that chair, they'd almost certainly run across the hideaway .38 in the ankle holster. In that case, I'd have to make a move and quick. And these were two armed cops, even if one of them was a fat idiot.

And Sykes was anything but an idiot.

So they set me in a folding chair under that same yellow cone of light as they went over by the big double garage doors and talked in whispers. They did not tie my ankles to the under-structure of the chair, and they left my tied hands in my lap. I guess I was their partner now. I knew part of their talk was exploring how they'd sell me out. I could have told them—I was going to die as soon as the thirty grand was in their hands. But I wondered if Dish Face would die, too.

Or maybe Sykes would explain how he was the superior officer and Dish Face had to settle for five grand. Might work. Five grand was a lot of cash, particularly for a dunce like Dish Face, who was used to playing Lou Costello to Sykes' Bud Abbott.

In about ten minutes a knock came at a door next to the garage doors. Sykes and Dish Face jumped a little, still in conference at the tool bench. The tall cop sent the fat one to answer it.

Two hoods strolled in, wearing dark topcoats with padded shoulders, dark pin-striped suits, striped silk ties, and pinch crown fedoras—you could buy a good used car with their combined clothing outlay. I'd seen them around, knew them by name but not well. The small one, Sal, had a toothpick he was working. The big-shouldered other guy, Vinnie, was chewing gum. They both looked bored.

Sal was in charge. The little guy is usually the smart one in these Mafia combos.

"You're Sykes?" he said to Sykes.

Sykes said he was Sykes.

Nobody asked who Dish Face was.

Nobody shook hands.

Rolling the toothpick around in his mouth, Sal walked over to where I sat and looked at me with no particular interest. "This is Hammer?"

"That," Sykes said, "is Hammer."

I wasn't gagged or anything, but no one asked my opinion.

The two New York guys seemed about as interested in their hosts as they were in the fish-glue boxes piled around the warehouse. But Sykes tried. He trotted out his smile, doing his best to keep the sneer out.

He said, "We can soften him up for you, if you like. Why work up a sweat?"

The toothpick roller had his back to Sykes. The gum chewer was several feet behind his companion, standing next to Dish Face.

Sal said, "No thanks. We can handle this." He worked his toothpick and reached inside his righthand topcoat pocket and came back with a roll of quarters.

"You boys wait outside," Sal advised his hosts.

Sykes shot him in the back of the head, and a bunch of what had been in it flew over my shoulder in a blur of red, white and green. So close to patriotic, yet so far. Sal made up for it, hitting the pavement and cracking the roll of quarters open, George Washington flying everywhere.

At the same time Dish Face whapped Vinnie hard on the side of the head with the nightstick. Vinnie spat out his gum and went down on the cement in a pile of confusion, not quite unconscious but not conscious enough to do anything about it, rolling on his back. Sykes walked over and Vinnie craned up just in time to see Sykes shoot him in the forehead. Vinnie's head went back and rested on a pillow of his own brains.

Sykes and Dish Face were facing each other with big smiles, the tall cop putting his revolver in its shoulder holster as he said, "You did fine, Sarge. You did good!"

That was when I sent my tied wrists down for the .38 and came back shooting, still in my chair, putting two slugs in Dish Face's fat gut. He flopped on his back like a speared fish on deck. He was whimpering and crying, hands clutching his bloody belly, squirts of red dancing between his fat fingers, autographing his cast. It would take him a while to die. That was the idea.

Meanwhile, Sykes was trying to decide if he had time to go for his shoulder-holstered rod. But he was smart. He had a calculating machine between his ears, and he added things up and said, "Good, Hammer. That makes us a fifteen-thousand dollar split."

"Right," I said.

I got to my feet. I surprised myself by how steady I was. Walked over to him.

Sykes bobbed a head at the scattered carnage. "Where should we dump the bodies?"

"I think right here is fine."

I kneed him in his remaining ball and he went down with a scream that kept going. I plucked the gun from under his arm and stuck it in my waistband, the butt cold against the bare skin of my shirtless stomach.

He was looking up at me, the pain subsiding. "Look, you… you keep the money. You just… just leave the clean-up to me. I can… I can rig this so we were arresting these two Mafia bums and things… things just got out of hand."

"Sounds about right."

Not a trace of smugness was in the long, angular face now. "Come on, Hammer. Killing me, what good does it do? I know when I'm beaten. Anyway, you can't kill me!"

"Why is that?"

"Damnit, man! I'm a cop!"

"Not really," I said, and shot him in the head.

CHAPTER THIRTEEN

The air hung thick with cordite. The floor ran red with blood, stippled with brains and general gore and an occasional quarter. I stepped around all that, careful not to slip in it or the vehicular oil, using a handkerchief to rub my prints off anything I'd touched, chiefly weapons.

Then I did a little cosmetic stage-managing, putting various guns in assorted hands to indicate a falling out, and shoot-out, among thieves. Well, among crooks and cops, if there was a difference in this town.

This should be the end of New York Mafia boys coming to Killing Town to look for Bob's thirty grand. This second round of fun included the two crooked cops who'd arranged things for both the Two Tonys and for Sal and Vinnie. And everybody was nicely dead.

And maybe now Carl Evello would understand how badly things could go wrong when you took on Mike Hammer. If he wanted more when I got back to the city, I'd be ready for round three.

My things were piled on the workbench, including my .45 in its shoulder sling, so leaving the .38 behind as part of the little melodrama I staged wouldn't leave me naked. I had my shirt, tie, suitcoat, raincoat, and hat, too. I looked damn near human, even if I didn't quite feel it.

By the time I was slipping out of the warehouse onto the waterfront street, where a cool foul wind was blowing in off the bay, a distant siren was wailing its mournful yet accusatory tune. Nice to know that even in this neighborhood, some good citizen had heard gunshots and called it in.

That gave me an idea, and I crossed to a little diner across the street and down a few doors, went in and ordered coffee. There was apple pie in one of those countertop four-tier displays, but it didn't look like your mother used to make, unless your mother made it runny.

So I settled for coffee and a booth by a window that hadn't seen a post-war cleaning yet. But through the smeary filth, I could see well enough, as a pair of squad cars rolled in with their sirens winding down and roof-mounted beacons glowing red. As the cops climbed out and went inside, pistols drawn, the red spotlights were left on, turning the officers satanic.

By the time a big black Dodge drew up, with no police markings but a blue-uniformed driver, I was on my second cup of coffee and asking myself, just how bad could that pic be? Then Chief Belden, in a topcoat and no hat hiding his unkempt thinning hair, left the black vehicle and entered the warehouse. He had the disheveled look of a man hauled out of bed on business. Nasty business.

I tried the pie. Answer: pretty bad. But I'd ordered it à la mode, and a scoop of ice cream is hard to screw up. Fifteen minutes later a glum-looking Belden came out, hands deep in his topcoat pocket. Standing in a bath of red light near a squad car beacon, he looked as if every inch of him was burning with rage, and his weed-patch head of hair seemed to have caught fire.

He walked out of beacon range and stood talking intensely with a couple of the uniformed officers, chest-thumping one and then the other with a thick forefinger. I dropped a buck on the booth's tabletop and went outside. The wind still stank but at least it provided some coolness.

I strolled over and came up behind Belden and tapped him on the shoulder. He turned his head, irritated—he'd been in mid-sentence—and when he saw me, it was like he spotted Banquo's ghost.

"A word?" I said, and nodded toward the diner.

He froze for a moment, as if waiting for me to be an unpleasant mirage that would just float away. When I didn't, he sighed and gave me the kind of reluctant nod he probably gave his wife when she asked him to take out the garbage.

I led him to the booth where my coffee cup hadn't been cleared yet, though the buck was gone. A skinny waitress came over and pretty soon both the chief and I had cups of coffee. He got a cigar going and then put it in an ashtray and promptly forgot about it.

"What the hell, Hammer?" he said. Even without the cop car beacon, his purplish, mottled complexion had plenty of red in it, and the pouchy eyes were runny and bloodshot. Who could blame him? Late Saturday night and something like this?

"Could you be more specific?" I asked.

"What the hell do you know about this, goddamnit?"

"Nothing really." I shrugged. "I just heard a rumor somebody shot Henny Sykes in the head."

His big hands were on the tabletop, opening and closing; hands, fists, hands, fists, hands…

"Let's back up, Chief," I said, raising a palm as if calling time-out. "Did you tell Sykes where to find me the other day? Because I had callers at the Charles girl's cottage."

The smile he gave me had little to do with the usual reasons for smiling. "Callers from New York? Who turned up dead on a back road this morning?"

I shook my head. "I wouldn't know anything about that, Chief. I'm not from here, remember? But you were the only person I told where to find me. Now, I like to think I'm a good judge of character. I got the impression you weren't a big fan of how Sykes conducted his police work. Was I wrong?"

"No."

"So you didn't tell him where I was. Did you tell anybody?"

His mouth tightened and a little embarrassment worked through the boiling rage. "Might have. Might have mentioned it. Not to Sykes."

"But somebody at the cop shop could've told Sykes. Would you say he was the Senator's man?"

He drew in a breath. Police chiefs don't like to be interrogated. They particularly don't like it outside a crime scene littered with bodies, half of which are cops'.

But he said, "I would not. Sykes has done the Senator's bidding, time to time, sure. But he works for anybody who can pay the price. *Worked* for anybody. He was dirty as hell, but he was connected."

"To the Senator."

Belden's shrug was barely perceptible. "Among others."

"Such as gangsters with New York ties?"

The chief's nod was also barely perceptible.

It was just as that reporter, Jackson, had said.

"I want to ask you a couple of questions," I said, lighting up a Lucky, then waving out the match. "I'll understand if you don't want to answer. But I'd appreciate it if you would."

"In about two seconds," Belden said, "the cuffs are coming out and *you'll* be answering the questions."

"That's your prerogative. But if you're implying I had something to do with that terrible tragedy across the street, you might want to consider what can of worms you'll be opening for you and your department."

His chin was tight and his mouth was, too. The eyes had all but disappeared into their pouchy settings. "Is that a *threat*, Hammer?"

I eased out some smoke. "Call it an observation. Here's another. You are free to haul me in on suspicion, obviously..."

"Because it's my prerogative," he said sarcastically.

"...but this time the gloves will be off, and I don't mean Sykes' favorite leather pair. I won't sit back and take it like a good boy. A powerful criminal lawyer in Manhattan will be my first call, and his first call will be to the top crime reporter with the *News*. Friends of mine on the NYPD, with their own Mafia connections, will roll into town and the investigation that follows will turn Killington inside out and upside down. Your call, Chief."

Hands, fists, hands, fists, hands, fists...

"Of course," I went on, "with Sykes gone, you could just go about the business of cleaning things up from within. That *is* the top cop's chair you're sitting in, back at headquarters, right? And the D.A. doesn't seem like such a bad sort."

Hands now. Just hands...

Quietly Belden asked, "What do you want to know?"

"Eva Charles says she was with her husband on the night of the Warburton girl's rape and murder. Is that an alibi you confirmed? Or was the word of any old Charles good enough?"

He didn't like the question, but he answered it anyway. "We checked it. Confirmed it."

"Where were they? At home?"

He shrugged. "Eventually."

"Well, that sounds like they were somewhere else for a while. What, out for supper? A movie?"

He shifted in the booth. "Lawrence Charles came in on the train and Eva Charles met him at the station, picked him up. They went home. That's all there is to it."

I was frowning. "What train?"

"The train from New York."

I leaned in. "Are you saying Lawrence Charles was on the same train as the murder victim?"

He nodded, but waved it off. "Yes, but they weren't traveling together. Lawrence had spent three days in New York at a convention for food cannery company executives. His father was there, too, but came home earlier in the day."

I was shaking my head. "Chief, Lawrence Charles and Jean Warburton may not have been traveling together, but you *do* know that she was his secretary, and by secretary, I mean she was laying him."

He gave me the non-smile again. "Hammer, we confirmed from witnesses that the wife was seen at the train station. Presumably she picked her husband up and took him home. We know that Jean Warburton was raped and strangled. Does that strike you as a husband and wife project? Like putting up the new blinds or painting the back porch?"

"Not exactly," I admitted.

"And why, if the Warburton girl was his mistress, would Lawrence have to rape her? She'd just been in New York for the cannery convention. What do you think she was doing with her boss in his hotel room for four days? Taking dictation?"

That sounded about right.

He leaned forward and spoke softly, just between us. "Hammer, I have no doubt you were framed. And I have no doubt the fine hand of the late Lieutenant Henry Sykes arranged it. But the sex pervert who did the crime was probably some bum passing through… and you fit that bill, and I can see the Charles family—either the Senator or his son or both—putting that frame around you to keep any public inquiry from dipping into the unpleasant fact of father and son passing that girl around between them like she was a dish of mashed potatoes. It's the kind of sick scandal that could take down a reputation, which even a man of the Senator's standing couldn't hold up. So you were just the fall guy. The patsy."

I sighed smoke. "Okay. Fine. I see all of that. But why did the Charles girl clear me? And why, besides my boyish charm, does she want to get hitched to me? And why, in God's name, did the Senator and his son and the daughter-in-law welcome me to the family like my last name is Vanderbilt?"

"You want an answer?"

"Hell yes I want an answer!"

"I have no damn idea." He got himself out of the booth and looked down at me with an expression that might be described as fatherly. Of course, so could the look on my old man's mug when he got out the razor strop.

"Hammer," he said, "why don't you find someplace else to be? Someplace that isn't just outside a multiple-homicide crime scene, for now. And by tomorrow? Someplace that isn't my town."

He finally remembered his cigar, reached in and took it, stood there and re-lighted it and did something that threw me a little.

He winked at me, and was gone.

Beat as hell, I got back to the hotel just after two a.m. I went into my room slow, with the .45 in hand, since after all it was no secret I was staying here. Right now I wasn't sure who might have dropped by to wish me unwell…

But nobody was waiting.

I locked myself in and stripped down. The tub had a shower set-up, but I felt like soaking, and made it nice and hot, turning the bathroom steamy. I gently soaped my wrists where they'd been bound, and massaged my shoulders and arms where they had been given the salt water taffy treatment. Then I leaned back and relaxed and started to try to think things through. I had even more pieces now—everything I needed to put the jigsaw image together.

Only I was too damn tired. My brain refused to do any hard work and, when I felt myself getting sleepy,

I crawled out and toweled off and climbed between the sheets stark naked. If the maid ignored the DO NOT DISTURB sign, that would be her problem.

The next thing I knew, somebody was knocking. Maybe it was the maid at that, because the knock was gentle, tentative. I looked at the bedside clock, and almost exactly twelve hours had passed—it was five after two, and afternoon sun was filtering around the edges of the shade I'd drawn.

Also on the bedside stand was the .45, and I stepped into my boxers and took the gun with me to the door. Because it might *not* be the maid...

I undid the bolt but left the night-latch and cracked open the door.

Melba's lovely face, bisected by the chain, looked at me with those gray eyes filled with concern, but the red wound that was her mouth had its corners turned up.

"Oh, Mike! I'm so glad to see you."

I let her in. That I was in my shorts with a .45 in my mitt didn't seem to register—she'd been around me enough to be used to that kind of thing.

"I know you wanted me to stay at home," she said in a rush, as she stepped into the room. The gray of her dress was darker than her eyes; with little black polka dots and a scoop neckline, it fit her like that green thing had back at the police station when she sprung me.

"But," she went on, "I was going stir crazy there, and just *had* to see you."

"Have you had lunch?"

"No."

"We can go down to the dining room or I can call room service."

"Let's stay here."

I called down, got dressed, and we sat beside each other on the bed and waited.

"I heard my father and my brother talking," she said. "I was so worried. They said that terrible policeman…"

"Sykes?"

"Sykes. That he and another 'unscrupulous' officer had been killed, and some gangsters from New York, too. And they think maybe you had something to do with it."

"What do you think?"

Melba let out a little laugh. "Well, of course you had something to do with it!" Then she frowned. "Are those New York gangsters just going to keep coming, Mike?"

"I think maybe I've discouraged them."

She sighed. "Good… But I'm beside myself, worried the police are going to come after you again. Maybe you should leave town. I can go with you if you like. If you even want anything to *do* with me now."

Room service came. The waiter set us up on a little table. I had a steak, baked potato and the trimmings with a beer. She just had a chicken salad plate with coffee. Always thinking about her figure. Who wasn't?

I put the trays of dirty dishes outside and when I came back, she was already half out of her clothes, stepping out of black pumps. She was no innate strip artist, like Jean Warburton in that sleeper car window; but she had a lot to work with, and just unveiling that creamy white body, set off by the white shoulder-brushing hair, the high full breasts, the narrow waist, the swell of hips, was enough to get me out of my clothes and under those covers with her in record time.

She liked it gentle and that's how it was again. Slow and sensual, a song starting sweet, gradually picking up tempo—the warmth of her mouth, the stickiness of the lipstick, the feminine fragrance of her—notes perfectly in tune, played exactly right, the rhythm building but never wanton, a loving, lovely melody ending on a high note.

We did as convention dictated and lay on our backs with the sheets draped under our shoulders and pillows propped behind us, and smoked our cigarettes—me a Lucky, her the girlish Marlboro. I'd been with my share of women, maybe more than my share, and often real beauties, like this one. But Melba was different. Special. A lot of women like it at least a little rough. Lust takes no prisoners.

But this flower could only respond to a gentle touch, and that was fine with me, as long as I could control my impulses, because the rewards were generous.

I had a feeling words romantic and sweet were about to come from the girl. Her expression, after all, was dreamy as her eyes looked skyward, or anyway ceiling-ward, following wisps of smoke doing a harem girl dance.

"I'm releasing you," she said.

"Huh?"

She turned toward me. Her mouth, lipstick gone, found mine and kissed me sweetly.

"Releasing you," she said. "I was wrong to demand such a price."

"Marrying you, kid, is a bargain."

She touched my face. "I shouldn't marry anyone."

"Why? There must be *some* poor slob out there looking for a beautiful blonde with millions of bucks. Maybe you aren't trying hard enough."

She smiled a crinkly little smile, genuinely amused, but the eyes stayed sad. "I'm not fit, Mike."

"Come on."

"No. I'm not. I'm… damaged goods. No man should have to put up with me. I admit I'm surprised that you… I mean, you're such a roughneck. Yet you do have tenderness in you."

"We need to talk about this."

"You being tender?"

"No."

"About… what, then?"

"About why you wanted to marry me. I think I know. No. I *do* know."

She shook her head, the blonde arcs of it swinging. "No. That's impossible."

I leaned on an elbow. "Well, let's start with the big picture. The undeniable part. You love your father, you love your brother, you love your family. They may be flawed, but all of us—most of us anyway—

learn to love our family despite the flaws. Will you accept that?"

She was frowning, as if I'd spoken in a foreign tongue. But after a few seconds, she nodded.

I went on: "Your father is covering up something about the Warburton girl's death."

She started shaking her head.

I shook mine back at her. "Honey, I know she was your daddy's mistress…"

"She was his secretary!"

"Right. His *private* secretary. And when he lost interest, or she got too demanding, he passed her over to your brother, who by all reports is a well-known rounder."

She looked away. But she didn't deny it.

"What exactly happened, I don't know," I admitted. "But your father, probably at your brother's urging, fitted me for the now-famous frame. They wouldn't have hung me on a wall, either."

Very quietly, she said, "They don't hang people in this state."

"I was speaking figuratively, honey. Now let's get literal. Let's get to why you wanted to marry me after you cleared me."

Her smile was a little too honeyed as she touched my cheek. "Mike, you're very sweet, but you don't know what you're talking about."

"I'm not sweet, and I do know. Your father or your brother did something—something to do with the

Warburton girl's death—that puts one or both of them at serious risk. But you're a good girl, a decent person, and you got wind of the frame-up and you couldn't stomach it. You couldn't be part of an innocent person going to jail and maybe the gallows... all right, the electric chair... even if you were just on the fringes, the sidelines."

Very softly she said, "Maybe... maybe that's true."

"Here's what else is true. The heart of it. The goddamn nub. *Clearing me made you part of the cover-up.*"

"That's simply ridiculous."

"No. You wouldn't have known to clear me if you didn't know about the cover-up, the frame. So that made you an accessory after the fact to murder and, yes, rape. Sooner or later I'd likely find that out. What other choice did you have? *A husband can't testify against his wife.*"

Her lips were quivering. Her eyes getting moist.

I said, "And I was going to get a ten thousand dollar pay-off for the privilege of being your husband on paper. But there would be no consummation. No fun and games. We kind of double-crossed ourselves on that account, didn't we, honey?"

She flung herself at me, her arms hugging me, her face buried in my chest, tears flowing. I let her do that for a while.

Then I eased her away and I held her eyes with mine.

I made my voice as gentle as I could. "Now, Mel... I need to ask you a few things, and it's not going to be pleasant."

She rolled her eyes. "Why, has *this* been pleasant?"

I smiled just a little. "Very pleasant, before we started talking. But every marriage has talk in it. It's not just fun between the sheets. And not all the talk is pillow talk."

She was sitting up in the bed, sheet gathered at her waist, her arms folded across her naked breasts. Her chin was lowered and she was shivering. It was not cold.

"Honey," I said, "I need to ask, and I need the truth. Is there anything about your father or your brother that would make you think one of them might be capable of rage? *Violent* rage."

She shivered some more. No answer. Not a nod or a head shake, either.

"I need to know, baby. Would either of them be capable of strangling another human being?"

She began crying again.

I put my hands on her bare shoulders. "Or do you already know? Was it your brother? Did *he* strangle that woman?"

She shook her head. It wasn't her saying no—it was, *I don't know.*

I felt like a heel, but I had to press on. "What about… I'm sorry, darling, I have to ask. What about rape? Is Lawrence capable of such a thing?"

She swallowed and she looked at me with eyes from which tears tumbled, her lovely face streaked with the stuff.

"Yes," she said. Her voice small but firm. "I *know* he is."

"Honey, how do you know?"

"That… that's how it *always* was with us," she said. "Growing up…"

CHAPTER FOURTEEN

I was in the library the Senator used as his office in the Colonial mansion atop the Bluff.

I'd left Melba at the hotel, not wanting her around when I had my little talk with her father, not even sure home was a safe place for her. The sun was down, the evening cool, with dark clouds chasing themselves across the sky while God's belly growled as if hungry for sinners to smite.

This time the patriarch of the Charles clan—casual in a loose-fitting tropical sports shirt, birds and flowers on a pale yellow background—was behind his boat of a desk. All he lacked was a captain's cap. I'd pulled a visitor's chair up. Though I'd said nothing specific about why I was there, he seemed to know instinctively that the comfy overstuffed chairs around the library's central coffee table, with its stack of bestsellers, were not appropriate.

And yet there *was* a social aspect—he had again summoned Eva to bring me a beer, though he already had a bottle of Old Grand-Dad going on the desk, half a tumbler of it before him when I came in.

Mrs. Lawrence Charles was also dressed casually at home on a Sunday evening—white short-sleeved blouse, navy slacks, open-toed sandals—but in full make-up that fairly screamed her naturally pretty features. She didn't even rate a "thanks" from her father-in-law this time, trundling in and out without acknowledging my presence.

"Sounds to me, son," he said, slurring a shade, "that you were a busy boy yesterday, after we spoke. I detect your fine hand in last night's waterfront doings, do I not?"

"You do," I admitted, and took a swig of Rheingold from a pilsner. "The festivities were held in a warehouse of yours, by the way. I wonder if that's significant."

His shrug was small yet exaggerated. He was pretty buzzed. "The late Lieutenant Sykes and I did business, time to time... but he was not doing my business last night."

"No, I figure he was just using that warehouse because he had access to it. Last night was about the money my army buddy stole from those New York hoods. They'll back off now that four of theirs are dead, with two dead coppers tossed in for good measure, adding some heat."

The broad-nosed face, with the bushy eyebrows and

pale-blue eyes, was home to an unsettling smile. "You do lead a lively life, son."

"Ernest, I seldom get bored." I sipped beer. Always good to be genteel in a millionaire's mansion. "But by now I think you'll agree that you could find a better husband for your daughter."

Another small yet overstated shrug. "Meaning no offense… you were *her* choice, not mine."

"You know, I believe that. You raised a decent daughter, Senator… and I'm going to call you 'Senator,' since I don't think the cozy son-in-law relationship is going to happen. Anyway, it just seems right."

He poured Old Grand-Dad. "Whatever pleases you, Mr. Hammer. And I would agree with your assessment—my daughter is a fine girl."

I nodded. "She is. I don't know if I ever will marry, but if I do, I could hardly hope for a better wife. She's smart, has a nice sense of humor and, like I said, she has a real streak of decency… which I'm a little surprised she picked up in this place."

He frowned, but his eyes were swimming. He drank more bourbon. "I don't believe insults are necessary, young man. Remember, you're a guest in this house."

"My apologies. But I'm not really a guest this evening—I just showed up and barged in."

"Point taken."

"Still, you did raise a wonderful girl, Senator. She learned that you and your son were going to stick me with a murder and rape charge, making it a cinch

I'd get a bus to Sing Sing and a one-way ride on Old Sparky. She couldn't abide that, so she pretended to know me, and got me a get-out-of-jail-free card. Only it wasn't free, really—I had to marry the girl. Now, there's a briar patch any sane man would jump into willingly. But why'd she do such a crazy thing?" I sat forward. "Because she knew she was an accessory to your crimes, and that if I married her, I'd never be able to testify against her."

His mouth worked for several seconds before anything came out. "I committed no crime."

"Maybe not. Maybe this is all your son. But I'll just bet you committed plenty of sins of omission." I waved a hand at the ceiling. "How could you not know that your precious boy was diddling his sister, *your daughter*, raping her night after night, again and again?"

He said nothing. He poured more bourbon, hand shaking, though he got it all into the glass.

I shook my head. "No, I won't marry your daughter. She's already released me. She knows me well enough now to understand I would never go along with this madness. Would you really sacrifice your daughter, and her future, to protect a son who is a rapist and a brute? A murderer?"

He looked at the glass in his hand. "Lawrence is... is no murderer."

"Oh? Well how about *you*, Senator? What was *really* going on between you and Jean Warburton? And how did your son fit in? Don't you normally pay your chippies off when you're done with them? Send them packing? Or is it typical of you to pass one on to sonny for sloppy seconds?"

"*Shut up!*" He pounded a fist on the desk. The tumbler jumped and some precious bourbon spilled. "Shut up..."

"What did the Warburton girl want from you, Senator? It must not have been money. Why did she go along with a hand-off to Lawrence?"

He was trembling. The great, powerful man was trembling. He gulped bourbon greedily, then poured and had some more.

"Senator?"

He sighed. His eyes looked past me at nothing. Or maybe everything.

"Mike," the Senator said, the familiarity back, rather desperately, "she wanted the one thing I wouldn't... *couldn't*... give her. Marriage."

"Was she pregnant?"

He shook his head. "No, she had something else to hold over me."

"What the hell could that be? Photographs, maybe?"

He covered his face and began to cry. Quietly at first, then racking sobs kicked in. I watched him, appalled and fascinated. This seemed way too human for a captain of industry.

"She knew," he said, "she knew... knew I... that I *loved* her."

And it came to me.

"She was going to meet *you* that night," I said. That was who her elaborate reverse striptease in the window had been about. "Tell me, Senator—was Lawrence in love with her, too? Was she about to throw your son over to go back to his daddy?"

He sighed, nodded, the ugly yet folksy face a streaky wet mask of tears.

"All three of you were in New York at that convention," I said. "She must have been shuttling between your hotel rooms, keeping both father and son happy! And Lawrence got wind of it. So he *did* rape and kill her! He followed her from the train when he saw she was all dolled up to go back to her sugar daddy. Little Larry was furious with both of you and so he dragged that girl into the bushes and he raped her and then he strangled her!"

"*Stop!*" he said. "Don't. You don't understand."

"Yeah, right, you loved her."

"You… you would have loved her, too, Mike."

"Yeah?"

"She was special… so very special." He gazed at the bourbon bottle. "…The best goddamn piece of tail I ever had."

I just looked at him. Nobody that big had ever looked so small to me.

Then I said, "Well, why didn't you marry her then? You're a widower, free and clear. Marry her and bang her till you're blue in the face."

"Hammer—you… don't… under… stand. My wife, my late wife, was a *Killington*."

"What?"

He sat forward in the padded swivel chair, a professor schooling a very slow student. "The Charles & Company Cannery was originally the Killington Cannery."

"After the town?"

"No, you fool! After the family the town was named for! My wife's father was the great-grandson of the Killington who started it all. That generation, there was no male Killington to carry on the family line."

"Okay. So your late wife was a Killington. So what?"

He was waving his hands, an out-of-control politician. "So I can *never* remarry! Are you mad? It would tarnish the family's reputation, disgrace the good name of our business! Bad enough that after Alice and I married, she agreed to put the company in our name. Now, so many years later, I would become the object of derision, the aging degenerate who married his young secretary. As if I would ever *consider* marrying a woman who came from the stock *she* did!"

I'd had enough of this creature.

I stood.

"Tell you what," I said. "I'll keep what I know to myself—for a price."

He was so drunk he could barely smile, but he managed. Contempt oozed from him like pus from a boil. "I should have *expected* that."

"Not the price you think." I leaned two hands on the desk. "Institutionalize Lawrence. Protect him from himself, and protect the world from him. Your daughter needs help, too, and I'll talk to her about it. There are plenty of good shrinks in Manhattan. But I want proof that you've put that chip-off-the-old-block away. For good. You're a powerful man. You can pull that off. I got faith in you, Ernest."

He was shaking. "Lawrence… Lawrence is next in line."

"If you really care about the future of your company and the family reputation and that crap, then stay healthy. Take vitamins or something, maybe lay off the cigars and Old Grand-Dad. You have grandsons upstairs, right? Just keep yourself breathing till one is of age. Maybe the kid won't grow up a monster—who knows? We got a deal?"

He looked at me, possibly wondering if he could arrange better assassins to try to kill me than the New York mobsters had, but finally nodded.

I went out.

In the entryway, as I collected my raincoat from a rack, I felt something prod my back gently.

"That's a gun, Mr. Hammer," Eva Charles informed me. "A little automatic I carry in my purse. But quite large enough to sever your spine."

She knew to reach around and get the .45 out from under my arm. Of course, she didn't have sense to switch her pea shooter with my cannon. I wished I'd had the sense to replace the hideaway .38.

"Outside," she said. Quiet but insistent. "We'll take the car you borrowed from my sister-in-law."

The fish-glue factory—Charles & Company Glue Works—was a modern-looking two-and-a-half-story building that might have been a grade school. Its brick was pale yellow and shiny, reflecting moonlight that peeked between the streaky dark clouds, rays that also danced on the bay the factory edged. The building had some size, but seemed insignificant next to the sprawling, ancient, prison-like cannery that also fronted the bay. The Charles & Company Cannery was twice as tall, three times as wide and four times the length of its offspring, its towering smokestacks like guard towers.

We pulled into a lot where only one other car was parked, her husband's sleek black Alfa Romeo. I had driven here with Eva keeping the tiny rod trained on me from the rider's seat. I had considered running the Packard into a telephone pole or maybe just snatching the midget automatic from the pudgy little broad's fat fingers, but for the former I couldn't work up the speed in town, and as for the latter, I could take that away from her any time, with some but not great risk.

Better to let this play out.

She had said nothing on the way, except "Turn here," and various other driving instructions. I had not been surprised that the factory was where we ended up. I got out of the Packard, and she and her gun directed me toward a side entrance.

As we went, the breeze whipped her dark slacks like flags and got under her loose white top and ballooned it, making a parody of her already considerable shape. The scene was eerie, with the water irregularly reflecting moonlight darting through the clouds, the threat of rain hovering like dark ghosts, the half heels of her sandals clicking on the slanted pavement of the parking lot.

She used a key with her left hand, unlocking the side door, and I skipped another chance to grab that little gun away. Maybe curiosity was going to kill a cat named Hammer.

We were inside one big high-ceilinged room that appeared to be the entire plant, which on Sunday was empty of workers. Eight open stainless steel vats, each nine or ten feet high, five or six feet wide, ran along the many-windowed wall on the bay side of the building. A wide area for worker access was between these vats with another eight, identical in height and width, on the opposite side, where a three-tiered catwalk overlooked the tanks, which were filled with a jelly-like liquid. Hanging from the ceiling, high above each vat, was a metal mixing device like a giant corkscrew drill.

Eva walked me up to the top catwalk tier, passing stacked boxes labeled alum, egg albumen, sulfurous acid, phosphoric acid and zinc, among other ingredients to season this sticky soup. There were stations over each vat with control panel sets of switches. At the end of the top catwalk, extending out a ways over the lower two levels, was a box-like enclosure constructed of the same black metal-work. She prodded me at the base of my spine with the gun and I made my way down to the door that said, LAWRENCE T. CHARLES, PRESIDENT.

She reached around me and knocked—again, an opportunity for me to wrest that rod away from her and I didn't.

The president himself answered.

Lawrence Charles had a stricken look, the vacation tan overtaken by flushed cheeks. The thing that gave me the creeps about this clown was how much he looked like Melba, the same long lashes and pretty gray eyes. His black hair was still slicked back, thirties gangster-style, but a few strands had come loose, like a spring that had slightly sprung.

She peeked around me and he frowned at her, somewhat petulantly.

He said, "I still don't see why you insisted on bringing him here."

She let out a disgusted little huff. "Where would you suggest?" she asked indignantly. "You were already here, working."

Then she handed him my .45 and he took it and trained it on me with a thin nasty smile, and I realized I may have misjudged the situation.

"Inside," he told me, backing up as he did, waving me in like a plane on a flattop deck.

Nothing fancy about the office. A row of file cabinets at right, a central modern-looking metal desk with piles of paperwork, a big window out on the plant floor, with blinds that could shut, as they were now.

But under that window was a very comfortable-looking couch, black leather, lots of padding, including the arm rests. I had a good idea that it was used for more than an occasional nap by the top glue company executive, and the faint smell of perfume suggested he may have spent his Sunday afternoon working on more than the papers on the desk.

Eva directed me to the visitor's chair. Lawrence got behind his desk, keeping the gun steady in my direction, and sat in his swivel chair, as if I was about to be interviewed.

She stuck the little gun in the back of my neck as she stood behind me, looking across at her husband. "He knows everything. We have to do something."

Lawrence frowned, devastated. "He *knows*?"

"Well… maybe not everything. But enough."

Only suddenly I did know everything.

I risked turning my head to look at her, just a little. "*You* strangled that girl."

She bonked me on the top of the head with the tiny rod. "Shut up. You don't know that."

"I'd ruled out a woman doing it, because the hands were too big. I saw the marks on the girl's neck at the morgue. But you've big hands, lady. You've got big everything."

"*Shut up!*" she screamed in my ear.

I ignored her and spoke to her husband. "Does your father know, Lawrence? That *you* loved her, too? She wanted to marry him, so he passed her to you, and then *you* fell for her like a ton of bricks. She must have been something in the sack. I watched her getting dressed for your old man." I whistled. "Something to see, all right."

"Sure you did," Lawrence said sullenly.

"No, swear to God. I crawled out from under a freight and I'm in Killington maybe ten seconds before I get a real old-fashioned eyeful. One of those reverse stripteases, like Lili St. Cyr, starting with the sheer stockings."

Eva conked me again.

"No," Lawrence said to her, holding up a hand. "Let's hear what he has to say. Let's see what he thinks he knows."

I accommodated him. "You were on the train, Lawrence—not sharing a compartment with the girl. You already had a feeling she'd been running a relay back at the convention hotel, between you and Daddy Fishbucks. Now you see her stepping off the train, dressed to kill. One look and you knew who she was going to meet. You followed her, you confronted her, and dragged her off into those bushes. You had your way with her, and your way is rough to begin with, and she was furious. She must have told you she'd go to Daddy and tell him what you'd done."

I turned just a little and smiled at Eva. She was the one with the stricken look now, the heavy make-up turning the beautiful features clownish.

"This is where you come in, sweetie. You came down to meet your loving hubby, a nice little surprise. I have a feeling you work pretty hard to try to show him he can have a good time at home and doesn't have to go after these cheap little tramps. You must have learned to like it rough a long time ago. But it's hard to compete with a beauty like Jean Warburton, who didn't deliver two boys to your man like you did. So you followed him, didn't you? *And you saw what he did.* Did it horrify you? Or did the punishment he dished out please you? Maybe excite you? Doesn't matter. What does matter is you heard Jean Warburton threaten your husband. Threaten to go to Daddy. Threaten to go to the cops, maybe. Rape charges are no picnic—take my word for it. Or maybe she would go to the papers—expose the whole sordid mess. The father and son whose idea of a promotion for a hardworking gal in the plant is a comfy couch in their private office. The son whose idea of lovemaking is forcing a female, hurting her, hitting her, raping her. The wife who has a weight problem and pretends not to notice when her husband steps out, and looks for other ways to be important to him. Like this one."

She had tears in her eyes, but I'm surprised they didn't freeze, as cold as her expression was.

"You strangled her, all right, Eva. But don't pretend

it was for your husband. It was very much for you. Just for you. And about time one of Larry's chippies made *you* feel good."

She started to strangle me now, but with the little gun in her hand, it didn't go anywhere, and Lawrence said, "Stop," and she did as she was told.

He could have stopped her that night, too, but he didn't. These two were a match made in hell.

Lawrence stood. "I'll get the boat."

She nodded. "We'll have to weigh him down. Bodies swell up and float. If they find him in the bay, this whole thing will start up again."

"We'll weigh him down, don't worry."

"Maybe we could just shoot him and dump him on a side road, and the police will write it off as part of these out-of-town gangsters killing each other."

Lawrence shook his head. "No, darling. Boat's better."

I said, "You know, it really isn't polite, talking about me like this. I mean, I'm sitting right here."

She cuffed my ear with the little gun.

"Hey!" I said, and gave her a dirty look.

Lawrence came around and jerked me to my feet. He had surprising power, but then he did have those broad shoulders on that skinny frame.

They took me out of the office and Eva led the way while Lawrence walked behind me with the .45 leveled at my back. Our feet clanged on the black metal floor of the narrow walkway. We were about halfway down the catwalk when I dropped to my knees, swung around and grabbed Lawrence by the knees and pitched him over the side.

He splashed into the jelly in the cooling vat and was floundering down there as Eva screamed, but instead of taking a shot at me, she leaned over the rail to see how much trouble her precious man was in. I jumped her and was trying to wrest the gun away, but she had weight and surprising strength going for her, and we did an awkward dance while Lawrence provided the music, splashing and screaming, in a gurgling kind of way.

Maybe the switch got thrown accidentally, when Eva and I bumped into it together, or maybe I threw it myself, to distract her, because that's what the near deafening whirring did as the giant drill bit came twisting down, and her eyes were big and watching the monstrous corkscrew when I shoved her over and sent her to join her husband.

She displaced some of the jelly but replaced it as well, and as I leaned on the rail, I noted the consistency of that yellow-green glop was really too thick to swim in. And yet they tried. They tried.

And all the while their eyes were on the giant descending mixing blade.

Finally it plunged in, a mammoth metallic phallus, and it took them down, whirling and twirling them as they shrieked in terror.

But the shrill screams of their discordant duet soon ceased, only a nightmare accompaniment remaining—electrical whirring, mechanical grinding, bones crunching, flesh ripping, the mucilage mixture bubbling and gurgling like a witch's cauldron, stripes of red circling, the gooey thick surface roiling with strange shapes beneath.

"Huh," I said.

The little woman got what she wanted, after all.

A husband who would stick by her.

ABOUT THE AUTHORS

MICKEY SPILLANE and **MAX ALLAN COLLINS** collaborated on numerous projects, including twelve anthologies, three films, and the *Mike Danger* comic book series.

SPILLANE was the bestselling American mystery writer of the 20th century. He introduced Mike Hammer in *I, the Jury* (1947), which sold in the millions, as did the six tough mysteries that soon followed. His controversial PI has been the subject of a radio show, comic strip, and several television series, starring Darren McGavin in the 1950s and Stacy Keach in the '80s and '90s. Numerous gritty movies have been made from Spillane novels, notably director Robert Aldrich's seminal film noir, *Kiss Me Deadly* (1955), *The Girl Hunters* (1963), in which the writer played his own famous hero, and *I, the Jury* (1982), which set the template for a decade of violent-crime-based action blockbusters.

COLLINS has earned an unprecedented twenty-three Private Eye Writers of America "Shamus" nominations, winning for the novels *True Detective* (1983) and *Stolen Away* (1991) in his Nathan Heller series, and for "So Long, Chief," a Mike Hammer short story begun by Spillane and completed by Collins. His graphic novel *Road to Perdition* is the basis of the Academy Award-winning Tom Hanks/Sam Mendes film. As a filmmaker in the Midwest, he has had half a dozen feature screenplays produced, including *The Last Lullaby* (2008), based on his innovative Quarry novels, also the basis of *Quarry*, a Cinemax TV series. As "Barbara Allan," he and his wife Barbara write the "Trash 'n' Treasures" mystery series (recently *Antiques Wanted*).

The Grand Master "Edgar" Award, the highest honor bestowed by the Mystery Writers of America, was presented to Spillane in 1995 and Collins in 2017. Both Spillane (who died in 2006) and Collins also received the Private Eye Writers life achievement award, the Eye.

MIKE HAMMER NOVELS

In response to reader requests, I have assembled this chronology to indicate where the Hammer novels I've completed from Mickey Spillane's unfinished manuscripts fit into the canon. An asterisk indicates the collaborative works (thus far). J. Kingston Pierce of the fine web site The Rap Sheet pointed out an inconsistency in this list (as it appeared with *Murder Never Knocks*) that I've corrected.

M.A.C.

Killing Town*
I, the Jury
Lady, Go Die!*
The Twisted Thing (published 1966, written 1949)
My Gun Is Quick
Vengeance Is Mine!
One Lonely Night
The Big Kill
Kiss Me, Deadly
Kill Me, Darling*
The Girl Hunters
The Snake

The Will to Kill*
The Big Bang*
Complex 90*
Murder Never Knocks*
The Body Lovers
Survival... Zero!
Kiss Her Goodbye*
The Killing Man
Black Alley
King of the Weeds*
The Goliath Bone*

For more fantastic fiction, author events,
competitions, limited editions and more

VISIT OUR WEBSITE
titanbooks.com

LIKE US ON FACEBOOK
facebook.com/titanbooks

FOLLOW US ON TWITTER
@TitanBooks

EMAIL US
readerfeedback@titanemail.com